THIS
BOOK
BELONGS
TO

MELISSA
ANNE
LIM

Star Girl

Henry Winterfeld

TRANSLATED BY KYRILL SCHABERT
ILLUSTRATED BY FRITZ WEGNER

A CAMELOT BOOK / PUBLISHED BY AVON BOOKS

AVON BOOKS
A division of
The Hearst Corporation
959 Eighth Avenue
New York, New York 10019

First Camelot Printing, March, 1976

CAMELOT TRADEMARK REG. U.S. PAT. OFF. AND IN
OTHER COUNTRIES, MARCA REGISTRADA, HECHO EN U.S.A.

Printed in the U.S.A.

Contents

Contents

Star Girl

HENRY WINTERFELD was born in 1901. He grew up in Berlin and started studying music. However, he soon decided that writing should be his profession.

Mr. Winterfeld now lives in New York with his wife, and divides his time between inventing toys and writing books for children.

One

A Little Girl Came Flying

Walter was the first to discover the girl. She was huddled at the foot of a tree, smiling uncertainly.

"There's a girl sitting here in the middle of the forest," Walter called to the others.

"What sits where?" croaked Otto, crawling on his hands and knees out of the thick underbrush of spruce trees where he had been cutting mushrooms. With a knife clenched between his teeth, he looked like an Indian on the warpath.

It had rained during the night, and the children had gone into the Hollewood to pick mushrooms. They had ventured much farther in than ever before, right up to the big clearing.

Walter's sisters, Gretel and little Lottie, came skipping down a knoll.

"Where is the girl?" Gretel cried breathlessly.

"I see her. I see her," called Lottie, and clapped her hands in excitement.

The strange girl had not moved. She was about seven or eight years old, with blonde hair that touched her shoulders and very big violet-blue eyes. Her skin was as white as snow. She was beautifully dressed. She wore a short red coat over a blue silk dress, a small red cap, blue socks, and blue velvet pumps. Around her neck hung a string of huge clear stones, which sparkled like diamonds in the sun. The girl looked like a little princess and did not seem to belong in this lonely, wild forest. There was a nasty bruise on her forehead, as though she had bumped her head badly.

"What is your name?" Walter asked politely.

"Mo," said the girl.

"That is no name," Otto said with an air of importance. He took his glasses out of his pocket, put them on, and looked sternly at the girl. She blushed with embarrassment.

"Is that your first name or your last name?" Walter asked pleasantly.

"My father's name is Kalumba," the girl said. She had a soft, melodious voice, but it seemed a bit awkward and foreign.

"How old are you?" asked Walter.

"Eighty-seven years," said Mo.

The children looked puzzled.

"Eighty-seven years?" Walter said slowly. "You mean seven or eight years, don't you?"

"No," said Mo. "I am eighty-seven years old. I know exactly. My birthday was eight days ago."

Walter scratched his head. "That seems funny," he said, and looked bewildered.

Gretel kneeled beside the girl. "Are you sick?" she asked.

"No," said Mo. "I am very fine."

"You have a bad bruise on your forehead," said Gretel. "Did you bump your head?"

"It doesn't hurt," said Mo. She thumped it firmly with her finger, to prove that it did not hurt.

"We must bandage it," Walter said. "Has anyone a clean handkerchief?"

Gretel and Lottie hadn't any at all, and Otto, reluctantly, pulled a big checked one out of his pants pocket. It looked rather grimy.

"Would this do?" he asked.

"No," said Walter.

"I have a handkerchief," said Mo, and from her coat pocket she took a large white one. She showed it to Walter. "It belongs to my father. He lent it to me because I had forgotten mine."

Together, Walter and Gretel tied the handkerchief around her forehead.

"There," said Walter. "That will keep the dirt out."

Mo looked at him gratefully.

"How did you happen to get here?" Walter asked. "Did you lose your way?"

Mo shook her head.

"Where are you from, anyway?" he demanded.

"From up there!" said Mo, pointing.

Walter looked up at the tall spruce. "From the tree?" he asked skeptically.

"Higher than that," replied Mo.

"Maybe you dropped out of the clouds?" Otto asked mockingly.

"Higher than that," said Mo.

"Still higher?" The children gasped.

"Perhaps she came in a plane," said Gretel.

Mo nodded eagerly. "Yes," she said.

"Did you really come by plane?" Walter asked in consternation.

"Yes," Mo said. "I came in a space ship."

"W-w-wi—with a space ship?" stammered Walter.

"Yes—with a space ship."

The children were speechless.

12

Two

A World-Shattering Event

The trees rustled softly in the wind. Somewhere in the forest a cuckoo called three times. With an angry chatter, a squirrel jumped from branch to branch, and from far away came the rumble of distant thunder. Then all was quiet again. The children stared at the little girl in amazement. After a while, Walter cleared his throat and asked, "Where are you from?"

"I'm from Asra."

"Asra—!" breathed Lottie excitedly.

"What is Asra?" asked Otto.

"Asra is a star," said Mo.

The children, without thinking, looked at the sky, but naturally in the daylight they could not see any stars.

"Are you perhaps from Mars?" asked Walter.

"I do not know what you call us," said Mo. "We call it Asra."

"But you look like a human being," said Otto suspiciously. He was suspicious by nature.

"We look very much like human beings," said Mo. "I learned that in school."

"But are you really eighty-seven years old?" demanded Lottie shyly. "That is the age of a grandmother."

"We stay young for hundreds of years," said Mo.

"Hundreds of years!" cried Gretel. "How old are your parents?"

"My parents are many thousands of years old," replied Mo.

The children looked dumbfounded. Even Otto was impressed, but he did not wish to show it and asked, "You're sure you're not lying?"

"What is that?" inquired Mo.

"You don't know what lying is?" piped Otto.

"No," said Mo.

"Lying," explained Otto, "is if you, for instance, steal a

cookie from the cupboard and then say you did not do it."

"I did not steal any cookie," said Mo. "I don't know what a cookie is."

"You don't know what a cookie is?" exclaimed Otto indignantly.

Gretel snapped at him, "Leave her alone! Perhaps they don't have cookies on Asra!"

"The whole world knows cookies," insisted Otto.

"Shame on you," cried Lottie. "Your behavior is disgusting."

"For Pete's sake, shut up!" shouted Walter. "A miracle has happened, and you are fussing about a cookie. If this girl is really from a different planet, this is a world-shattering event."

"Yes, yes, a world-shattering event," squeaked Lottie, and excitedly hopped from one foot to the other.

Walter solemnly turned to Mo. "My name is Walter Brenner. This is Gretel, and this is Lottie. They are my sisters. This is my friend Otto. We salute you and bid you a warm welcome to earth." He extended his hand with ceremony. Mo seemed bewildered. Apparently she did not know that she was expected to shake Walter's hand.

"Good day," she said with a friendly smile, which revealed a row of pearly white teeth. In his embarrassment Walter withdrew his hand and stuck it into his pants pocket.

"Did you arrive in a space ship all by yourself?"

For the first time Mo gave a gay laugh. It sounded like the voice of a lark.

"Oh, no," she said. "That would be impossible. I came with my father."

The children looked around in fright.

"Where is your father?" asked Walter.

"My father went back to the Moon," said Mo.

"To the moon," shouted the children.

"I thought you came from Asra," Otto challenged with a frown.

"Oh, yes," said Mo. "We do come from Asra. We stopped off on your Moon. My father's friends gave us an escort with their space ship as far as the Moon. They are waiting for us there until we return from the Earth. Then we will all fly home together."

"Where is your mother?" asked Lottie eagerly.

"My mother is visiting on another planet," answered Mo.

Now all the children were talking at once. "What are your space ships like?" "Are they flying saucers?" "Are they big or small?"

"Our space ships are very beautiful," said Mo. "They are round and silvery."

"Do you use rocket propulsion?" asked Walter.

"Or atomic power?" chimed in Otto.

Mo placed her finger on her nose and seemed to reflect seriously. Then she said, "I don't know about such things. I'm just a little girl. It has something to do with magnetism, I think. Once my father tried to explain it to me, but I couldn't understand."

"Why didn't you fly back to the moon?" asked Gretel.

"How could I?" said Mo, laughing gaily again.

"Why not?" demanded the children.

"I fell out of our space ship by mistake," said Mo, chuckling.

"Fell out?" screamed the children. "Tell us. Tell us. How did it happen?" They sat down in the grass beside Mo and stared at her in fascination.

Three

There Are Good Human Beings

"Well—it happened this way," Mo began. "I begged my father to take me along to the Earth. I wanted to visit your planet. My father, you know, had told me so much of Earth —about the deep seas and high mountains, the great forests, the old-fashioned cities . . ."

"How does your father know so much," interrupted Walter, completely amazed.

"My father is a grand master of Earth science," continued Mo. "He has studied about you for many thousands of years. He also has been here several times and collected stones and plants for our museum."

"Why didn't anyone see him?" asked Otto.

"He always landed in secret," said Mo, "in some lonely region, and only if it was still a bit dark. We wanted to land today, just before sunrise, on a large, open plateau, but something went wrong with the landing gear, and we kept hovering low over the forest. 'We cannot land,' said my father. 'We will have to return to the Moon.'

" 'Oh, what a pity!' I said. 'It looks so lovely down there.' I was looking out of a porthole because I was anxious to see. I had never seen such funny trees. Our trees are quite different—but yours are nice too," she added tactfully.

The children listened entranced. Gretel's bow had come undone and her unruly curls hung over her face, but she did not notice it. Walter and Otto, hands clasped around their knees, bent forward without moving. Lottie was kneeling close to Mo and never took her eyes off her.

"What a beautiful necklace you have!" she said admiringly.

"My father gave it to me for my fiftieth birthday," said Mo. "My friends all get chains like this."

"Are the stones made of glass?" asked Walter.

"I do not know," answered Mo. "There are lots of stones like these on Asra."

"Don't always interrupt her," objected Gretel, impatiently pushing back her hair. "Please continue," she begged.

"I leaned out quite far," Mo went on, "to get a better look, and my father called 'Be careful. Don't lean out so far. Remember, here on Earth you weigh much more than at home.' 'Yes, Father,' I said, 'I'll be careful'—and then I tumbled out."

"Oh, how dreadful," cried Lottie.

"I fell on top of a tree and clung to it.

" 'Mo, where are you?' my father called. 'Where are you? I can't see you.' My father stuck his head out of the porthole.

" 'I fell out,' I shouted.

" 'Yes, I noticed that,' my father called. 'But where are you? I can't see you.'

" 'I'm sitting on a bar with a lot of prickly green needles,' I shouted.

" 'Are you hurt?' Father called.

" 'No,' I said. 'I am well.'

" 'I can't help you,' my father called. His voice became more and more distant. Our space ship floated higher and higher.

" 'What shall I do, Father?' I called. 'How can I stay alone on Earth?'

" 'Climb down the tree,' my father shouted through a loud-speaker. I could scarcely see him.

" 'Hide in the woods until it gets dark. Immediately after sunset, walk toward Asra until you come to a large, open field. I will pick you up there tonight. Be sure to be there. We will have no time to spare. We will have to return to Asra at once.'

"After that I couldn't hear him any more. The space ship vanished."

Mo fell silent, and the children looked at her full of sympathy.

"Did you cry?" asked Lottie, her voice choked with emotion.

"What is cry?" asked Mo naively.

Lottie was completely taken aback. She opened her mouth but could not speak.

"How did you get down from the tree?" asked Walter.

"I climbed down from one bar to the other and finally jumped," said Mo.

"Was it then that you bumped your head?" asked Walter.

Mo nodded and gently touched the bandage around her forehead.

"Why did your father order you to hide in the woods?" inquired Otto.

Mo hesitated and gave the children an anxious look.

"My father told me that there are many bad human beings," she whispered.

The children could not think of anything to say.

"There are also good people," Walter said finally.

"Oh, yes," agreed Mo quickly. "My father knows that. But he says that you have not yet reached the point where we can be friends."

"Your father doesn't think much of us, does he?" growled Otto peevishly.

"But you're not even afraid of *us*, are you?" asked Lottie.

"We are *good* human beings," Walter reassured her.

"You look awfully nice," said Mo. "You won't harm me, will you?"

"I promise!" replied Walter.

"What does that mean?" asked Mo.

"A promise is when I give my word of honor to do as I say," explained Walter.

Mo seemed comforted.

"What are you going to do if your father does not come for you this evening?" Otto wanted to know.

"My father said he would," said Mo.

"But if he doesn't?" insisted Otto.

"Oh, that would be awful," said Mo, frightened, "because he could not return for another fifty years."

"Why?" chorused the children, puzzled.

"I don't quite know," said Mo. "The Earth has to be in one spot and Asra in another, otherwise we could not fly here and back, my father said."

"But your father flew back only as far as the moon?" asked Walter.

"Yes," explained Mo. "He has to fix his space ship in a hurry."

"To the moon!" cried Otto in amazement. "Then how can he be back by this evening?"

"Why, that is not so far," said Mo and smiled.

"And you're going to stay all by yourself in this forest until tonight?" asked Gretel with concern.

"Well, I'm supposed to," said Mo quietly.

Excitedly Walter jumped up. "Nothing doing! You can't!" he said with determination.

"Why not?" asked Mo, looking surprised.

"There are wild beasts," said Otto.

"What are wild beasts?" asked Mo.

"Wild beasts are wild beasts; they bite," said Otto.

Mo began to look worried. "We don't have wild beasts," she said shyly.

"Don't you have any animals at all?" Lottie wanted to know.

"No," said Mo. "Nobody bites at home."

"There will be a thunderstorm," said Walter, scanning the sky with concern. A fat, black cloud looked menacing. There was the sound of distant rumbling, this time much louder than before.

"What a funny noise," said Mo uneasily.

"That is thunder," explained Gretel.

"Thunderstorms are awful," said Lottie. "There is lightning and then thunder and so much noise that you have to cover up your ears."

Mo looked at the children in bewilderment.

"What shall I do?" she said sadly. "I don't know anybody on Earth!"

"You'll come home with us," said Walter firmly. "I won't allow you to stay all alone in the forest until tonight."

Otto jumped to his feet. "Why your house?" he asked crossly and pushed back his glasses, which had slid down his nose.

"I was the first to discover her, that's why!" snapped Walter sharply.

"Oh, you!" cried Otto angrily. "I saw her too, except I didn't holler my head off. Our house is much nicer and bigger than yours."

"Your house is NOT nicer than ours!" shouted Lottie in indignation.

"And you never have enough to eat!" insisted Otto. For a minute, he had completely lost his temper; otherwise he would not have said it. Gretel went for Otto like a tigress and would have scratched his face if Walter had not intervened.

"Otto is a liar!" she shrieked, her eyes sparkling with fury. "We always have plenty to eat."

"Oh, let him shoot off his mouth," said Walter appeasingly. He was the oldest and most sensible among them.

"No!" cried Gretel. "Mo will come with us. Lottie and I can take care of her. Girls get along much better with each other."

23

"Yak, yak," jeered Otto. "Girls fight worse than boys."

"Shut up," roared Walter menacingly, and Otto kept quiet.

"If you can't get along, I'll knock your heads together," Walter continued.

Even Gretel kept quiet. She was hard to tame, but she had great respect for her brother.

"Now you are no longer so pleasant," said Mo, frightened.

"You see!" chided Walter. "You've frightened her!"

"Why did you shout so?" asked Mo.

"You needn't be afraid," said Walter soothingly. "Otto always blows up like a turkey. But he's a good guy in spite of it."

"Where I come from nobody blows up," said Mo. "We children are all fond of each other."

"I guess on Asra you're all angels?" Otto said in a surly tone. But he was already a bit embarrassed.

Walter paid no attention to him. "Do you want to come with us?" he asked Mo. "My parents would be happy to meet you." He could be very polite. His parents were poor, but they had brought up their children to be well mannered. He offered Mo his hand to help her. She grasped it, and he pulled her up. She looked at him. She was much shorter than Walter, though taller than Lottie. "Will you bring me back here tonight?" she asked.

"Of course," said Walter. "We can't wait to see the space ship."

"Oh, yes!" cried Lottie, enthralled. "Please, please!"

Mo looked solemnly at Walter. "Promise," she said.

"I promise," said Walter.

"Promise that you keep your word to do as you say," she insisted.

"I give you my solemn promise that I'll keep my word," swore Walter and raised his hand.

Now Mo was satisfied. She took off her coat, shook out the loose grass and spruce needles, put it on again, and straightened out her silk dress. "Do I look pleasant for your parents?" she asked Gretel.

"You look very elegant," said Gretel and blushed. She herself was wearing a cheap cotton dress, no stockings, and worn-out sandals. But instead of being jealous, she felt nothing but great admiration for Mo.

Lottie was enchanted. "You are as lovely as a fairy," she exclaimed.

"What is a fairy?" asked Mo eagerly.

Lottie wanted to go into a long explanation, but Walter would not let her. "We must go," he warned, "otherwise we'll get caught in the storm."

He led the way through the forest, and the others followed along. Gretel took Mo by the hand, and Lottie traipsed excitedly behind. Otto brought up the rear. He was still miffed and whistled to himself as though he wanted no part of it all. Suddenly he stopped and shouted, "The mushrooms! I left the mushrooms under the tree!"

Unconcerned, Walter walked on and called, "We won't need them. We're bringing home something far more exciting than mushrooms. It will be a sensation when we return with Mo!"

"Yes," shrieked Gretel triumphantly. "We shall be rich and famous, and all our neighbors will envy us." She quickly turned around and stuck out her tongue at Otto.

Four
Are Cows Animals?

The children ran along the last part of the trail until they reached the county road. There they took their bicycles out of the bushes, where they had hidden them before they went into the forest.

"I am full of stones," said Mo, and leaned against a tree. She panted like a puppy that had run too hard.

"Are you feeling sick?" asked Lottie.

"Your air is much thicker than ours," said Mo. "At home I can run faster."

"Do you want to rest?" asked Walter.

"Oh, no, I am quite fine," said Mo. She looked at the bicycles in amazement. "What do you do with those?" she asked.

"What do you mean?" answered Walter. "Those are our bikes."

"Our teacher told us that we had bikes in ancient days," said Mo. "I saw one in a museum."

"Museum!" protested Otto, quite hurt. "My bike is the latest model, with freewheeling and gearshift."

"At home all children have little airplanes," said Mo.

"How I'd love to have one," exclaimed Lottie.

The children pushed their bikes out on the road. Lottie did not own one and had to sit on the crossbar of Gretel's.

Walter's bicycle really belonged to his father, and Gretel's was an old girl's bicycle that an aunt had given her.

Again Walter anxiously eyed the thunderclouds that were looming above the treetops. "Let's go," he ordered.

"Must I run by your side?" asked Mo, worried.

"You'll sit on my crossbar," said Walter. Mo quickly ran up to him, and he helped her on. Then he pushed off and started to pedal. The wind blew in short heavy gusts, and he had to pump with all his might. "Are you comfortable?" he asked, panting.

"It is just a bit hard," said Mo.

"Lean against me!" said Walter.

Mo leaned against him. "That is better," she said happily.

"Some day when I earn money, I'll buy myself a motor bike," said Walter.

The golden strands of Mo's hair blew against his face, but it did not seem to bother him. "It's a long way to Asra, isn't it?" he asked.

"Oh, yes, it took a long time to come," said Mo.

"Then you won't come back?" asked Walter.

"Perhaps, yes," said Mo. "But then you will be very old, won't you? My father said that humans get old fast."

"I won't be old for a long while," protested Walter. "After all, I'm only twelve now."

"At that age I was very small," said Mo.

They left the forest behind and reached the open meadow. By the side of the road ran the Hollebrook, gurgling gaily. To their left were giant boulders, and to their right were broad meadows extending to the distant mountains. Cows were grazing in the fields.

Mo called out laughingly, "What kind of funny humans are they? They have four legs!"

"Those aren't humans," said Walter. "They are cows."

"Are cows animals?" asked Mo.

"Cows are domestic animals," replied Walter.

"Do they live in a real house?" asked Mo.

"In the winter they live in a barn," answered Walter.

By now he was puffing hard, as the wind was blowing half a gale. He looked around to see whether the others were following. Gretel and Otto were close behind. Gretel's brown curls were whipping around her ears, and Otto was hunching over his handlebars like a racer.

"What for are cows?" demanded Mo.

"For milking," explained Walter. "Milk is something very good."

All that, apparently, was Greek to Mo. She looked around with mounting astonishment and said finally: "The Earth is peculiar." Gretel and Otto had finally caught up with Walter and were pedaling beside him.

"How are you doing?" Gretel called to Mo.

"Fine!"

"Do you like it?" shouted Lottie.

"I like it," answered Mo. She was feeling happy. The earth seemed to please her a lot. But suddenly she looked startled and called, "Who is that?" Three children, two boys and a girl, were running toward the wall from the side of the Hollebrook. They jumped up the embankment and blocked the middle of the road.

One of the boys waved his arms excitedly and called merrily: "Yoohoo, yoohoo."

"Are those children too?" Mo asked timidly.

"Yes," said Walter. "They are good kids and friends of ours." He put on his brake and came to a halt. Gretel and Otto stopped too. Willy and Erna were twins. Both had red hair and lots of freckles. Konrad was fat and had tight brown curls. All three were barefoot.

"Come and help us catch trout," Willy suggested.

"We have no time," said Walter. "We have to get home in a hurry."

"It's still a long while until lunch," said Konrad. He was hard to understand as he was busy sucking a caramel.

"We have more important business than lunch," hinted Otto mysteriously. Willy at once was all ears. "What?" he called expectantly.

"We've had a terrific experience," said Walter.

"Yippee!" cried Willy, fidgeting excitedly. "Shoot; let's hear, let's hear!"

Erna eyed Mo from head to toe. "Who's she?" she asked, and frowned.

Mo was equally perplexed. It so happened that Erna was wearing shorts, just as boys do, a striped sweater, and a Tyrolean hat with a feather cocked at an angle. Her two thick red braids stuck out saucily beneath the hat, which really belonged to her brother.

"That is Mo," said Gretel excitedly. "We found her in the Hollewood—can you imagine?"

"In the Hollewood?" growled Konrad unbelievingly. "She looks like a city slicker to me!"

"Don't be fresh," flashed Lottie indignantly. "She is from Asra!"

31

"Never heard of it," mumbled Konrad.

"She is from another planet," said Otto proudly.

Willy and Erna gaped and Konrad almost swallowed his caramel. Dumbfounded, they stared at Mo.

Suddenly Willy came to life. He jumped high into the air and shouted, "Boy, oh boy! At last something really exciting has happened. Did you see her land in a flying saucer?"

"Unfortunately, no," said Walter. He told them what had happened. "Mo is flying off tonight, and we are going to take her to the spot," he added.

"We'll come too," shouted Willy, tugging at his pants, which had slipped down when he jumped.

"I don't know . . ." said Walter reluctantly. "May they come along?" he asked Mo.

Mo nodded her consent.

"Yippee!" yelled Willy.

"May I touch her?" asked Erna tensely.

"You may shake her hand," Walter said generously.

Erna offered her hand, but Mo merely looked confused.

"You, too, must give her your hand!" said Walter. "That is what people do here on earth. It means that one is friendly."

Obediently Mo took Erna's hand and pressed it timidly.

"What a delicate hand she has," said Erna admiringly.

"I want to shake her hand too," begged Konrad.

"Not you," said Walter. "Your hands are dirty." Konrad looked at his hands with a puzzled expression. "They're always like that," he murmured.

"Why are you taking her home with you?" Erna wanted to know.

"Because we can't leave her alone in the woods," Gretel replied.

"Our parents will be surprised," chirped Lottie in ecstasy.

"Take us along," called Willy. "We left our bikes at home."

"Nothing doing," said Walter. But then the storm broke, and it started to rain.

Five

Rainbow on the Horizon

"I am getting all wet," Mo called in astonishment.

"We'll have to seek shelter somewhere," said Walter, hurriedly glancing around. "The barn there," he called. "Let's go!" He took Mo by one hand, and with the other he pushed his bicycle. They hurried across the field to the barn. Willy and Erna ran ahead to open the barn door. Hardly had the children taken shelter when the clouds opened in a torrent of rain.

"Lucky," said Walter smugly.

The barn inside was dusky; there was the smell of hay and manure. The children sat down on bales of hay and gazed out at the rain. They left the barn door open to have more light. As the wind was blowing from the other side, they did not get wet. There was no letup in the lightning, and with every thunderclap Lottie shrieked "Eeks, how terrible!" and plugged up her ears. Hailstones pounded the roof, and the children all grew silent. Mo sat down next to Walter and did not move. Her mouth was half open, and her violet-blue eyes seemed bigger than ever. Each flash of lightning revealed her snow-white face and her silken blonde hair in an eerie light.

Gretel whispered to Erna, "Isn't she beautiful?" Erna nodded and unconsciously tugged her thick red braids.

At last the thunder grew fainter and the rain abated. "It will soon be over," said Walter. "Were you afraid?" he asked Mo.

"A little bit," she said. But then she laughed, jumped up, and walked around in the barn. She gently touched the wooden walls, eagerly inspected an old plow, and then sniffed the hay. This made her sneeze, and with a fright she sat down on a milking stool.

"Hay smells good," said Willy with a grin.

"It smells nicely," said Mo. "Are those your beds?" she asked.

"What do you mean?" asked Walter, perplexed.

"Is not this your house?" Mo asked.

Konrad and Willy burst into laughter, but Walter turned on them furiously. "Watch yourselves, you fatheads. Mo has never been on this earth. You wouldn't like it either, if they laughed at you on Asra." Then, turning to Mo, he said, "No, this isn't our house. We're in a barn."

"Do cows live here?" she asked.

Willy and Konrad started to giggle again, but Walter gave them a dirty look, and they became silent at once.

"Do you have houses too?" asked Gretel.

"We have very nice houses," said Mo.

"Oh, do tell us!" chimed the children.

Mo watched them out of the corner of her eye, as though she did not quite trust them, but gradually became livelier. "Our houses are all silvery, big and round, and during the day they turn with the Sun. Each house stands in a park with blooming trees and lovely lawns. Our trees are different. They are thick and all alike, and their leaves are a bluish white. There are flower beds on the lawns. The flowers have a pretty glow. They also glow at night like small colored lanterns. When the wind blows, they give out a gentle hum, as though they were singing. Some sound like chimes; others moan like an organ. At night, often we go outside and sit in the grass for hours and listen to them. Everywhere in our parks there are swimming pools with waterfalls, fountains, slides, and swings. The children have little submarines in which we dive below. We steer them through lighted tunnels and wide grottoes and over beautiful pictures painted on the bottom. Then we shoot to the surface, jump in the water, and swim as long as we feel like it. We also have many playgrounds where we can land in our planes. There we have merry-go-rounds and reading rooms, TV screens and small palaces—just for us children. We play all day." The children listened spellbound. Erna had her arms slung around her knees, and Willy snickered once more. Lottie, completely enthralled, was hunched forward, biting her fingernails, something her parents had strictly forbidden. Otto's spectacles hung at the tip of his nose, but he didn't notice it.

"But when do you go to school?" he asked.

"Our school is an especially nice park," Mo continued. "We always have three days school and three days off. At school, we sit under tall trees in the shade of their big leaves. We like our teacher very much, but she can be quite strict when we don't study."

"But what do you do in the winter?" asked Gretel.

"What is winter?" asked Mo.

Otto adjusted his glasses and said: "Winter is when it snows and when the trees have no leaves."

"My fingers are always frozen in the winter," complained Lottie.

"On Asra it is always warm," said Mo. "The sun shines all the time. Only sometimes there are small pink clouds in the sky."

"Doesn't it ever rain?" asked Willy.

"Is that rain?" said Mo and pointed outside.

"Yes," called the children.

"We don't have that," said Mo.

"But you have water?" said Walter.

"Oh, yes!" exclaimed Mo. "Our water comes from the mountains. The tops of our mountains are all ice. We have canals, which bring the water from far, faraway mountains. Quite often we children take our speedboats up the canals, higher and higher; then we turn around and hurry home. Oh, what fun!"

"Boy!" exclaimed Willy. "I'll bet."

"But you have it good on Earth too," said Mo consolingly.

"Sometimes we play hooky," said Konrad with a bad conscience.

"I never do," exclaimed Lottie. "Now we have vacation." She was very proud about being in school already.

"Do your parents give you permission to drive the speedboats to the mountains all by yourselves?" Gretel asked.

Mo was surprised. "But that isn't anything bad," she said. "We children on Asra can do all we wish."

"Then you never get a spanking?" Otto called out.

"Spanking?" Mo asked in growing amazement. "What is that?"

"Spanking is if you get your backside slapped," said Otto. Mo eyed him, dumbfounded.

"Don't pay any attention to him!" Walter said hastily. "He's just envious."

"Do you go to church?" Erna wanted to know.

Mo smiled cheerfully. "Why, yes," she said. "Our church is as big as a mountain. It is made of transparent marble. Its roof is of silver and its tower of gold. The bell is as big as a house. We can even hear it up in the mountains, when we are very, very far away. Then we fly back in our planes to go to church. Sometimes we are many thousands of children. We all sing in the choir. That is very nice and solemn. What is that?" she called suddenly and stared outside, her eyes wide.

There was a rainbow on the horizon. The sun had pierced the clouds, and the rain had changed into a fine drizzle.

"That's a rainbow," said Otto. But he did not go into any further explanation because he was not quite sure himself what caused a rainbow.

"That is nice," said Mo admiringly.

Walter, lost in thought, was chewing on a blade of grass. "Asra must be beautiful," he murmured to himself.

"Don't you ever get bored?" asked Erna. "I get awfully bored sometimes."

"We always have a lot to do," explained Mo. "We fly all over Asra and visit other children. Each year we have a great children's festival on our artificial moon. . . ."

"Artificial moon!" Willy interrupted her excitedly. "You have an artificial moon?"

Mo nodded. "We don't have a Moon like the Earth. Our grownups made one themselves, just for us children. There we meet each year and have games. We also put on plays and dancing contests. . . ."

"Can you dance too?" asked Gretel anxiously.

"I've won a prize," said Mo proudly.

"Oh, please, please dance for us!" begged Lottie.

Mo jumped up, ran to the middle of the barn, and began to dance. She did a pretty pirouette, making her little silk skirt stand straight out. She performed graceful leaps like a real ballet dancer and hummed a strange yet gay tune. At

the end she dropped to one knee and held out her arms in a charming gesture.

The children applauded gleefully.

"You dance marvelously," exclaimed Gretel.

"I wish I could dance too," called Lottie.

"Dancing isn't so hard," growled Konrad. "I dance very well."

"You?" cried Willy. "You dance like an elephant in a circus. Look at me!" He jumped on the milking stool and was about to execute a daring turn when he got trapped by his own feet. He fell flat on his nose. The others doubled up with laughter. Only Mo was upset. She knelt beside him and asked anxiously, "Are you hurt?"

Willy sat up and grinned. "Me?" he said. "I've even fallen off a roof without getting hurt!"

"That's not true," shouted Erna angrily.

"It is *too* true," yelled Willy.

"It has stopped raining!" Walter interrupted cheerfully.

They ran out and looked around. The sun was shining, and the rainbow had paled. Meanwhile, the field had turned into a swamp. Konrad, Willy, and Erna waded across; the others had to take off their shoes and socks. "Shall I too take off my shoes and stockings?" Mo asked hesitatingly.

"That won't be necessary," said Walter. "I'll carry you." He put his arms around her, lifted her up, and carried her to the road. He was a strong boy, but even so he was flushed from the effort. Next he fetched his bicycle. He helped Mo up and was about to take off, but Willy held on to him and asked, "Couldn't you really give us a lift? We would like to be there when you arrive at your house with Mo."

"Full up," said Walter with determination.

"I could stand on the spur of Otto's hind wheel," said Konrad.

"How do you like that!" pouted Otto indignantly. "Both my tires would blow!"

They took off, and Willy, Erna, and Konrad stared after them with disappointment written on their faces. Walter pedaled furiously, leaving a spray of raindrops in his wake.

Six

Too Many Thrillers?

The children rode through the town, a sleepy little place in the lonely Holle Mountains. They stopped in front of a small house that stood at the end of Holle Road and rested their bikes against a fence. The house was tiny and unpretentious, but it was colorfully decorated, and flower boxes with geraniums adorned the windows. Rambler roses were climbing up the walls of the house, which stood in a small field with a few fruit trees. The smoke rising from the chimney on the red roof was a signal that the noon meal would soon be ready.

"Is that your house?" asked Mo.

"Yes," said Walter, self-conscious because it was the smallest house in the region.

"It is pretty," Mo said.

"Really?" exclaimed Gretel, relieved.

"We have such roses too," said Mo and pointed to the arbor roses. She seemed very happy to have discovered something familiar on earth.

The children were a bit exhausted from racing home. Gretel looked flushed and wind-blown, and Otto rubbed the calves of his legs with a groan.

"Are your parents good people?" Mo asked anxiously.

"They are very good people," smiled Walter.

"They won't do me harm?" asked Mo.

"You needn't be afraid!" said Walter. "Come." He took her by the hand and walked her toward the house.

Lottie, unable to wait, had already run ahead. She burst into the kitchen, all agog, and shouted: "Mummy, Mummy! We've found a girl from a different world."

Mrs. Brenner, who just then was standing at the stove cooking potato soup, turned in astonishment. "What did you find?" she asked.

"Gretel said we will be rich and famous, Mummy!" shrieked Lottie.

Walter and Gretel entered with Mo. Otto followed. He took off his cap and with it shielded the front of his jacket, as he had torn off a button when he was looking for mushrooms. Otto liked to be neat.

"Yes, Mom!" said Walter. "Just imagine! We found a girl in the forest who comes from another planet!"

"She is eighty-seven years old!" Gretel exclaimed breathlessly.

"She comes from Asra," shouted Lottie.

All this at once was too much for Mrs. Brenner. She was a good mother and adored her children, but she did not like to be fooled.

"Who is the child?" she asked.

Mo looked around in astonishment, as though she suddenly had been transplanted into fairyland. The fire in the stove, the old rocking chair, the rickety couch against the wall, the table and chairs, all these intrigued her greatly.

"Her name is Mo," said Walter.

"The child is well dressed," said Mrs. Brenner. "She must have rich parents. Where is she from?"

"But, Mom!" exclaimed Walter. "We just told you, she is from another planet."

"She has never been on earth before," said Gretel, her cheeks flushed with excitement.

"Her father is on the moon!" shrieked Lottie.

Mrs. Brenner eyed each child suspiciously, but all she saw were innocent and excited faces. "Max," she called, "please come here!"

"Where's the fire?" a voice responded from outside, and Mr. Brenner appeared at the back door. He was smoking a pipe and was holding an ax, having just chopped some kindling for the stove.

"The children insist that they have found a little girl in the woods who came from another planet," said Mrs. Brenner.

"Kids find all sorts of things in the woods. Did you also find mushrooms?" he asked mockingly.

"I found a lot of mushrooms, but Walter said I should leave them under the spruce," said Otto reproachfully.

"Well, that will make the rabbits and deer happy," said Mr. Brenner. Then with a start he asked his wife incredulously: "Did you say the children found a girl from another planet?"

"It's true!" said Walter. "She arrived this morning in a space ship."

"That is a world-shattering event!" screamed Lottie.

"She is taking off again tonight, and we shall take her there," said Gretel.

Mr. Brenner smiled. "Why, you really have thought up something entirely new this time," he said.

The children were baffled. Gretel impatiently pushed her curls back, eyes sparkling. "Father," she cried, "you don't by any chance think that we are lying?"

"Oh, no," answered Mr. Brenner. "It's just that you've read too many of those thrillers lately." Then he became serious and said, "There are no human beings on other planets."

"There are too!" shouted Lottie angrily.

"There are canals on Mars," explained Otto, eying Mr. Brenner over the top of his glasses with the air of a professor.

"They say there are flying saucers!" Walter added.

"Did you see her arrive in a flying saucer?" asked Mr. Brenner.

"No," said Walter.

"She fell out of her space ship by accident," chirped Lottie.

"She fell on a tree and then jumped down. She told us exactly how everything looks on Asra," said Gretel.

"The child told you that?" asked Mr. Brenner.

"Yes," cried the children.

Mr. Brenner pointed with his pipe at Mo. "Is she the one from another planet?" he asked.

"Her name is Mo," said Lottie.

"Come here, child." Mr. Brenner beckoned Mo. She was startled. Lost in thought, she had been admiring the squat kerosene lantern that hung from the ceiling. Frightened now, she looked at Mr. Brenner.

"Why don't you put the ax down, Max!" said Mrs. Brenner.

"Of course, yes," said Mr. Brenner, and put it next to the back door. Then he sat down on a chair, leaned forward, and smiled at Mo. "Do come here, child! I won't harm you." Walter nodded to Mo encouragingly. She walked up to Mr. Brenner and timidly said, "How do you do?"

"The child is a beauty," whispered Mrs. Brenner. Mr. Brenner offered Mo his big, callused hand.

"The Lord bless you, my child," he said.

Mo quickly grasped his hand and bravely tried to shake it. "Are we now friends?" she asked.

Mr. Brenner took a few vigorous puffs on his pipe. "Of

course we are friends," he said. "I love children. Now, tell
me, where are you from?"

"Why do you belch smoke?" asked Mo.

"Hm," said Mr. Brenner, startled. "I'm smoking a pipe.
Doesn't your father smoke too?"

"Nobody belches smoke at home," said Mo disapprovingly.

"Everything is different on Asra!" said Lottie. She placed
herself close to her father and anxiously watched his face.

"Asra?" said Mr. Brenner. "What is Asra?"

"Asra is a planet," said Walter. "Mo doesn't know what
we call it."

"So you're from a different planet, my child?" said Mr.
Brenner.

Mo nodded eagerly. "We stopped on your Moon," she
said.

"Is that right?" said Mr. Brenner. "Have you ever been
on earth before?"

"No," said Mo.

"And you arrived this morning?" he asked.

"I fell out," said Mo, a bit ashamed.

Mr. Brenner slumped back in his chair and crossed his
arms. "If this is the first time you've been here, how then
do you speak our language so well?" he asked, smiling
shrewdly.

Mo did not answer. The children were taken aback. In
their excitement they had never thought of that. How
could Mo speak their language? Nervously they stared at
her.

Seven

The Child Is Sick

Mr. Brenner waited patiently for Mo's answer. Finally he said, "Well, child, can you answer me?"

Mo eyed him with distrust. "Promise," she said suddenly.

"Promise?" Mr. Brenner was surprised. "What should I promise?" he asked.

"Nobody is supposed to know," said Mo, looking worried. "Promise that you will not break your word."

"I promise," said Mr. Brenner with good humor.

Mo bent forward and whispered to him. "My father has been secretly on Earth several times. He speaks many of your languages. We can also listen to your radios on Asra."

Mr. Brenner blinked a few times but remained silent.

"He agreed to take me along on this trip only if I learned your language," continued Mo. Then she wrung her hands and sighed. "My, it was difficult. I studied very hard, but it took me twenty years before my father was satisfied." She nodded earnestly.

"Twenty years—!" said Mr. Brenner, and again forgot to draw on his pipe. "How old are you really, my child?"

"I am only eighty-seven," said Mo modestly.

"Only eighty-seven!" murmured Mr. Brenner and frowned. "Just imagine! But why did your father want you to learn our language?" he asked.

Mo hesitated and rubbed her nose. Finally she said, "So we would not give ourselves away in case we ran into human beings." She laughed merrily and stood on her toes to peer over Mr. Brenner's shoulder.

"But that is funny," she exclaimed. "Who is that?"

The Brenners' fat black tomcat had sneaked in by the back door. He stretched himself, sat down with care, and stared at Mo without moving. The children laughed.

"That is our cat, Philip," explained Gretel.

Lottie ran to take him in her arms and brought him to Mo. "You may pet him," she said.

But Mo was afraid. "Is that too an animal?" she asked.

"Yes," said Lottie.

"Does he bite?" asked Mo.

"Philip only scratches at times," said Walter. "But he is a kind animal."

Mrs. Brenner walked up to her husband, clasped her hands over her apron, and looked at him inquiringly. "Max, who is the child? Where is she from? And why does she tell all that?"

"The child is sick," said Mr. Brenner. "Her hands are hot. She probably has fever."

"You think she is delirious?" Mrs. Brenner asked with concern.

Pensively, Mr. Brenner scratched the back of his head. "Looks that way; she doesn't seem quite all there," he said softly.

Mrs. Brenner looked at Mo, frightened. "Why does the child keep that kerchief over her head?" she called to her children.

Lottie dropped Philip and rushed up. "She jumped from the tree and banged her head," she called.

"Aha," said Mr. Brenner, and gave his wife a meaningful nod.

"Let me have a look!" said Mrs. Brenner, and undid Mo's kerchief. "Oh, dear," she cried, "that does look nasty!" She went to the sink, returned with a damp cloth and soap, and carefully cleaned the wound. Mr. Brenner brought some adhesive tape and gauze and put in on Mo's forehead.

"Does it hurt?" he asked.

"No thanks," said Mo nicely.

"Do you feel ill?" said Mrs. Brenner.

"Mo is not sick!" said Walter uneasily.

"She even danced for us," said Lottie.

"Are you hungry?" Mrs. Brenner asked Mo.

"What is that?" queried Mo.

"Would you like something to eat?" asked Mrs. Brenner.

"Do human beings eat too?" inquired Mo with interest. Mrs. Brenner nodded.

"We eat a pill, one a day," said Mo, "and each morning we drink the juice of blossoms. It keeps us healthy."

"We have potato soup with bacon dumplings!" said Lottie with fervor.

"What is potato soup and bacon dumplings?" asked Mo.

"Something awfully good!" insisted Gretel, proudly glancing at Otto.

"Louise," said Mr. Brenner firmly, "we cannot give the child any food. She has a concussion and should be in bed."

"But, Max," said Mrs. Brenner excitedly, "we can't just keep a strange child here and put her to bed. The child has lost her way, or maybe she ran away from home. I'm sure her parents are already desperately looking for her."

The children had been listening with mounting astonishment.

"Her father is on the moon!" shouted Lottie, close to tears.

"Her mother is visiting on another planet," shouted Gretel. Mr. and Mrs. Brenner paid no attention.

"Max, you had better take the child right to the police station," said Mrs. Brenner resolutely.

The children were horrified. "No, no, no," they cried. Even Otto was upset.

"We promised to take her into the forest tonight," pleaded Walter. "Right after sunset we are supposed to keep walking toward Asra until we reach a big, level clearing. That is where her father will pick her up in a space ship!"

"But, children," said Mr. Brenner, "do you really believe that this girl—just like that—has arrived from another planet?"

The children were beside themselves.

"Yes!" Walter yelled furiously. Never before had he dared to yell at his parents, and he immediately was very sorry he had.

Mr. and Mrs. Brenner were no less taken aback. "You

surely are a trusting soul, son," his father said, shaking his head.

Now Otto intervened courageously. "Couldn't we first take Mo into the woods?" he proposed. "Then we will see whether her father comes or not. If he comes, we will know that he comes—I mean, if he doesn't come, we will know that he is not coming and . . ." He gave up, feeling rattled. This didn't often happen, for Otto was smart. He was at the top of his class.

"Rubbish," said Mr. Brenner. Otto was hurt.

"Please, oh, Father, please," implored Gretel and Lottie.

"The child must go to the police station," repeated Mrs. Brenner with determination.

"But, Louise," said Mr. Brenner, "the police station is no place for a sick child! I'll go to the town hall and tell them that the child is with us." He was trying to put on his jacket, but Gretel and Lottie hung on to him and cried, "Daddy, Daddy! Please don't!"

"What do you say to that?" Mr. Brenner asked his wife smilingly.

"The children are crazy," sighed Mrs. Brenner. Mo had been forgotten in all the excitement.

"When do human beings eat?" she asked shyly.

Mr. and Mrs. Brenner turned around and looked at her in amazement. At this moment a number of voices could be heard outside, and then someone impatiently knocked at the door. Philip, the cat, shot under the couch like lightning.

Eight

Where Is That Monster?

There was more knocking, this time more violent.

Mrs. Brenner quickly took off her apron and pushed the hair back from her forehead. "Who can this be?" she said to herself.

The door flew open, and Willy and Erna were the first to bounce in. "Yoohoo!" cried Willy, and waved merrily at the children. Behind them several neighbors were crowding through the door, and wedged in among them was Konrad, perspiring and shoving with his elbows. "You're crushing me!" he cried angrily.

"Where is that monster from Mars?" called Mr. Hofer, Konrad's father.

"Does it wear a helmet? Does it wear a helmet?" shrieked Miss Beck, and almost craned her neck out of joint.

More and more people poured in. "Where is it? We want to see it too!" they shouted. Outside, people were even peering through the windows. In no time the small living-kitchen of the Brenners overflowed with excited neighbors.

"My goodness," exclaimed Mr. Brenner. "We are being invaded!"

The children, alarmed, had withdrawn into a corner.

Mo frantically clutched Walter's arm. "Who is that?" she asked, her eyes wide.

"They are our neighbors," whispered Walter.

"Are neighbors too human beings?" asked Mo.

"Yes," said Walter abruptly.

"Has it got a helmet?" Miss Beck piped up again.

"Now, you good folk," called Mr. Brenner. "What goes on here?"

"If you don't mind, Brenner," said Mr. Hofer, "we, too, would like to see the thing that arrived from Mars."

"Who told you that?" asked Mr. Brenner.

"My son Konrad told us that a small, female goblin fell

out of a flying saucer and that your children brought it home," said Mr. Hofer.

"Where is it? Where did you hide it?" voices wanted to know.

"Holy cow!" shouted Mr. Brenner scornfully. "The lad is off his rocker. There is no goblin hidden in this house! This is the girl my children found in the forest! See for yourselves!" He pointed at Mo.

"Oh!" said the neighbors—then silence. Mr. Hofer scratched his head. "But that is a real little girl," he said disappointedly.

"That's nothing from Mars, not on your life," declared Mr. and Mrs. Langmueller.

"She is so; she's from Asra," peeped Lottie.

"And I imagined something with a long, pointed nose, huge ears, and a bald head!" shrieked Miss Beck indignantly. A few people chuckled. The truth was that Miss Beck herself had a pointed nose and big ears, and, as everyone knew, she wore a wig.

"Konrad!" said Mr. Hofer ominously. "Come here, my lad! What sort of a cock-and-bull story did you tell?"

But Konrad stayed beyond arm's length as a matter of precaution. "I can't help it," he mumbled. "Walter said she came from another planet."

"That happens to be right," asserted Walter.

"Our kids, too, told us that a being from another planet had arrived," chorused Mr. and Mrs. Langmueller, who were the parents of Willy and Erna. The Langmuellers always spoke at the same time and almost always said the same thing.

Willy grinned blithely and Erna snapped, "Mo said herself that she comes from Asra!" Erna had changed her clothes at home. She was now wearing pretty shoes and stockings and a plaid dress. She had even loosened her thick red braids and let her hair drop to her shoulders, just as Mo wore hers. Willy was wearing the cap and feather now.

"What a cheap hoax!" cried Miss Beck, and raised her long, thin finger at Erna.

Erna sniffed disdainfully. By now, the neighbors had grown very embarrassed about pushing into the Brenners' house so unceremoniously. The men puffed their pipes in silence, exhaling thick clouds of smoke. The women stared curiously at Mo.

"Where is the child from, Louise?" asked Mrs. Reuter, a gray-haired woman with a kind face.

"That we don't know," said Mrs. Brenner regretfully. "She insists she is from another planet."

"The child is mad," declared fat Mrs. Paul. "You can tell by her eyes, right away."

"Mo is NOT mad!" Walter shouted furiously.

"I'm sure she escaped from an institution!" shrieked Miss Beck.

"She did NOT escape from an institution!" shouted Gretel, eyes sparkling with fury. "Her father is coming for her tonight."

"That child is from the city," insisted Mrs. Reuter emphatically. "She is much too elegant for Kummersville. Her parents must be rich. Her dress is made of pure silk."

"These are not my regular clothes," Mo said modestly.

"At home we wear much more beautiful clothes that are made of spun gold."

"Did you ever hear the like of it?" jeered Miss Beck. "If she isn't a little comedian!"

"If the child has lost her way, the police ought to be notified," a voice came from the background.

"Quite right," murmured the men, and nodded in assent.

"I planned to do that too," Mr. Brenner said, "but the child is sick. I was going to the town hall to report that my children had found the child in the Hollewood."

However, there was no longer any need of that. A strong, deep voice bellowed from the doorway, "What goes on here? What's the reason for this assembly?" Chief police sergeant Jacob Klotz was forcefully elbowing his way through the crowd. "Step back, step back!" he snapped, and the neighbors respectfully gave way.

Nine

A Fortune Round Her Neck

"What goes on here?" the policeman asked again, looking about severely.

"My children found a little girl in the forest, Chief," said Mr. Brenner. "She must have lost her way."

"Is that the girl?" asked the police sergeant, staring at Erna.

"Not me!" called Erna, growing pale.

"No, this one here," said Mrs. Brenner, and took Mo by the hand.

"Ah," said the policeman. He pushed a chair to the table, sat down, and laid his visor cap in front of him. Then he pulled a notebook out of his pocket and whipped out a pencil.

"What's your name?" he asked Mo.

"Her name is Mo!" said Gretel. The children had hastily flanked Mo as if to protect her.

"I didn't ask you," said the policeman harshly. Gretel glowered at him. The children could not stand the police sergeant. He was very tall and had a potbelly. His face was puffy and red, and he was bald. He always scolded them when they bicycled on the sidewalk of the little town.

"Can't you speak for yourself?" he asked Mo.

"You are very fat," said Mo.

"Hm," growled the police sergeant. "Some people are fat and some are thin. What's your name?"

"We don't have fat ones," said Mo.

Mr. Brenner cleared his throat noisily. "Look here, officer," he said.

"You will speak when you are asked!" the sergeant snapped at him. "First I will interrogate the child, then you. What's your name?" he asked Mo for the third time.

Mo remained silent, eying him suspiciously.

The policeman took a deep breath. "I won't eat you," he said. "I just want to help you. That's what I'm here for.

60

You want to get back to your parents as quickly as possible, don't you?"

"Oh, yes!" cried Mo hopefully.

"There, you see!" said the sergeant, pleased. "Here, my child"—whereupon he produced a lollipop from his briefcase and pressed it into Mo's hand—"that is for you."

"What is that?" Mo asked, surprised.

"That is a lollipop," said the sergeant. "Haven't you ever seen a lollipop before?"

"I have not been here very long," said Mo.

"What?" asked the policeman, stupefied.

"What do you do with a lollipop?" asked Mo.

Konrad snatched it from her, put it in his mouth, and sucked it eagerly. "You suck it," he told her, smacking his lips.

The sergeant took out a huge, checked handkerchief and wiped the perspiration from his neck. "The candy was not for you," he admonished Konrad.

"I just wanted to show her . . ." murmured Konrad, frightened.

The sergeant took up his pencil again and looked at Mo.

"First name!" he said, assuming an official air.

"I know nothing about it," said Mo, confused.

The policeman sighed. "What do your parents call you?" he asked.

"Mo," she answered.

"Last name!" said the sergeant.

"Her father is called Kalumba," answered Walter quickly.

The sergeant wrote it down in his notebook. "That is a

foreign name. Are you from a foreign country?" he asked Mo.

"You are wearing a funny suit," said Mo with much interest.

"That's a uniform," said the policeman with emphasis.

"Nobody has a uniform at home," said Mo.

"Look here, Chief . . . !" Mr. Brenner began again.

"Thunder and lightning!" shouted the policeman angrily. "Don't keep interrupting me all the time! I know my job here! I'll find out all right where the child comes from. How old are you?" he asked Mo.

"She is eighty-seven years old!" shrieked Lottie.

"Brenner," shouted the sergeant, "will you see to it that your children do not butt in constantly!"

Once more he mopped his brow and asked Mo, "In what year were you born?"

Mo put her finger on her nose and seemed to figure intensely. "In the year fifty-three thousand nine hundred and twenty-five," she finally said, with a sigh of relief.

The policeman put down his pencil and leaned back.

"Tell me, do you go to school yet?" he frowned at her.

"Oh, yes," said Mo.

"*Where* do you go to school?" he asked intently.

"Our school is beautiful," said Mo. "It stands below high trees in a park."

"Is that so?" said the sergeant. "In what town?"

"No," said Mo.

"What?" yelled the sergeant.

"We do not have towns," said Mo.

"Then it's in the country?" he asked.

"Oh, no," said Mo.

The neighbors started to giggle.

"Silence!" demanded the officer. "Where do you live?" he asked her hoarsely.

"On Asra," said Mo proudly.

"There, you see!" said the sergeant with an air of accomplishment. "Now, at last we're getting somewhere." He made more notes and then asked, "What's the name of the place where you live?"

"We don't have a place," answered Mo.

"No place?" queried the sergeant, raising his eyebrows. "You must live somewhere?"

"We live in a house. Our houses are round and silvery, and during the day they turn with the Sun. They stand in a park with trees, and the trees are quite different. . . ."

"Do you live with your parents?" the policeman interrupted impatiently.

Mo nodded.

"Where did you see your parents for the last time?" he asked.

"I did not see my parents for the last time," said Mo, looking worried.

The sergeant groaned. "Where are your parents?" he asked.

Mo looked at him suspiciously but kept silent.

"Don't you have parents?" he inquired.

"Certainly," said Mo, troubled. "I was in the forest, my father was looking out of the window . . ."

"In what forest?" asked the sergeant tensely.

"In the Hollewood," called Walter and Gretel.

"In the Hollewood?" said the sergeant with surprise. "Your father was looking out of the window? Did you run away from him?" he asked.

"No, I fell out," Mo said gloomily.

"Ah!" exclaimed the policeman, relieved. "You fell out of a car, didn't you?"

Mo did not answer.

"Why didn't your father stop?" he asked. "Didn't he notice that you fell out?"

"I don't know what that is," said Mo softly.

"You don't know what?" said the sergeant perplexed.

"Car," replied Mo.

The sergeant opened his mouth and then shut it. His face was bathed in perspiration.

"What then did you fall from?" he asked, feeling exhausted.

"From our space ship," said Mo.

The policeman was speechless.

Suddenly Mo was all laughter. "You have a lot of water on your forehead!" she exclaimed.

"Chief," Mr. Brenner called determinedly and, walking up to him, whispered in his ear: "The child is not all there. She keeps saying that she is from another planet."

"How? What?" the sergeant murmured. Then he exploded. "Why didn't you tell me that in the first place!" he snarled. "Of course, that will make my investigation very difficult. Insane! Thunder and lightning, that's a fine kettle of fish." He stared at Mo undecidedly.

"Sir, if you please," Walter said pluckily, raising his hand just as in class. "Mo really comes from another planet. Believe me, Mo isn't lying. She told us exactly what it is like on Asra, tonight . . ."

"Shut up!" roared the officer. "I have no time to listen to fairy tales." All the time he was looking at Mo with an air of perplexity.

"Ahem," he growled, "perhaps something is engraved on the clasp of her necklace. Name or address. . . . You have a lovely necklace, child," he added, all sweetness. "May I look at it?"

Mo raised her head willingly so that he could take a closer look.

"Could I hold it for a moment?" he asked as amiably as his gruff voice would permit.

"No," answered Mo.

"Why not, child?" asked the sergeant.

"You don't need a necklace," said Mo.

"I'll give it right back to you," the sergeant assured her.

"You have to give me your word of honor to do as you say," Mo said solemnly.

"Sure, sure!" said the sergeant in utter resignation.

Mo gave him her necklace, which he examined on all sides. "Unfortunately there is nothing on it," he murmured. Suddenly, he looked startled and stared incredulously at the big, sparkling stones. He weighed the necklace in his hand with mounting amazement, then turned and called, "Borgmann, lucky you're here. Come quickly."

Mr. Borgmann was Otto's grandfather. He was short, with a white, pointed beard. He also wore glasses. "At your service," he answered eagerly.

"You're a watchmaker, aren't you?" asked the policeman.

"Precisely," said Mr. Borgmann. "I repair pocket watches, cuckoo clocks, and I also fixed the steeple clock of our church."

"You know something about precious stones, don't you?" the sergeant wanted to know.

"Surely," said Mr. Borgmann. "I worked years for a jeweler in Wellerberg."

"Then take a look at these stones! Are they glass?" the sergeant asked. He squinted his eyes and handed over the necklace.

Mr. Borgmann pulled a magnifying glass from his coat pocket and carefully examined the stones. Suddenly he dropped the necklace on the table as though he had burned his hands. "Great Scot!" he stammered. "Those . . . those are all genuine diamonds!"

"Oh!" exclaimed voices from all around the room. The neighbors tried to crowd around the table all at once.

"Step back! Step back!" commanded the sergeant. "Or I'll have the room cleared." They stepped back.

"Borgmann, you couldn't possibly be mistaken?" asked the officer tensely.

"As sure as I am standing before you, sir!" asserted Mr. Borgmann, his voice choked with excitement. "These are the biggest and purest diamonds I have ever seen in my life! The necklace must be worth a million at least!"

"One million," murmured Mr. Brenner in a daze.

"One million!" gasped the neighbors, the men even forgetting to puff their pipes.

"Jumping Jupiter!" exclaimed Mr. Brenner. "One just doesn't hang a million around a child's neck!"

"Max, Max!" called Mrs. Brenner, beside herself. "I told you right away to take the child to the police station!"

The children, too, were amazed.

Only Mo did not seem to understand why everybody was so excited. "May I have my necklace back?" she asked meekly. Nobody answered her.

There was a dead silence except for the ticking of the clock and the bubbling of the potato soup that simmered on the stove. The rays of the afternoon sun slanted through the window and fell on the necklace lying on the table. The big diamonds sparkled like fireworks. Everyone was staring at the necklace, then at Mo, and back at the necklace.

"Where did you get that necklace, my child?" asked the sergeant finally.

"I'm sure the child stole the necklace and then made off with it," shrieked Miss Beck, looking around triumphantly.

"That's not true!" protested Walter and Gretel, enraged.

"Quiet!" ordered the policeman. "Is this necklace yours?" he asked Mo.

She nodded eagerly. "My father made me a present of it for my fiftieth birthday."

The sergeant heaved a deep sigh and motioned to Walter. "Where did you find her in the Hollewood?" he asked brusquely.

"Under a tree," said Walter.

"Tree! Tree!" scorned the policeman. "The Hollewood is huge. Under what tree?"

"Under a spruce tree," said Walter.

"It happened this way . . ." Otto reported solemnly. "I discovered a lot of mushrooms under a spruce tree. Suddenly Walter yelled, 'There's a girl sitting here in the middle of the forest!' I too had seen her, but Walter claims he saw her first. . . ."

"Where? *Where* did you find her?" the sergeant shouted at them.

"As we told you, under a tree," said Otto in a dour voice.

The sergeant grunted. "How did you get to the tree?"

"We walked," said Gretel.

"We took the Easter path," explained Walter. "We walked deeper and deeper into the forest until we came to a clearing. There Mo was sitting under a tree."

"All right, all right, under a tree," groaned the policeman. "Did you see anyone nearby?"

"No!" chorused the children.

"Did you by any chance hear anything suspicious?"

"I heard a cuckoo!" cried Lottie excitedly.

"There was thunder," said Gretel.

The sergeant got up with a jerk, put on his cap, and grabbed the necklace. "You will come along with me," he said to the children.

The children were struck with horror.

"May I have my necklace back?" asked Mo.

"No," said the sergeant. "I have to confiscate it. Can't let you run around with it. You'll risk your life."

Mo eyed him for an instant in utter bewilderment. "You are not a good human," she said furiously. With the speed of lightning she snatched the necklace out of his hand and, before anybody could stop her, darted through the back door and ran away.

"Halt! Stop!" roared the policeman and started after her. Unfortunately Philip, the cat, chose that same moment to sneak out. The sergeant tripped over him and, potbelly and all, landed in a mud puddle in the back yard.

Ten

Flat on Her Nose

"Good heavens!" exclaimed the neighbors, and all rushed outside to pick up the sergeant, but the children lit out the front door. Only Lottie could not make it. Her mother grabbed her in the nick of time and held onto her. The children could hear Lottie yelling: "Oh, Mummy, Mummy! I want to see the space ship too!" Then they ran out on the street and looked around for Mo.

"There she is!" shouted Willy.

Mo was running down the Holle Road like a hunted deer. Her hair flew out behind her like a weather vane.

"Mo! Mo!" screamed Walter. "Wait!"

But Mo did not hear him and already was tearing across the tracks of a grade crossing.

"Mo! Mo!" yelled the children, running after her.

"I've had it!" groaned Konrad.

"Do you want to be pulled in by the police?" shouted Walter.

"No!" snapped Konrad, and pushed ahead with his fat little legs.

"We're catching up with her!" called Willy triumphantly. "She can't run as fast as us."

Just as they reached the railway crossing, the gates came down, right in front of their noses. Walter and Willy wanted to climb over them, but the guard roared at them, "Get back! Get back!" shaking his fist. At that moment, the little train came rattling around the bend, and with much puffing and clanging the engine went chugging by. The train was going very slowly because it was going uphill. All the children could do was to stand helplessly behind the gates.

"What a tough break," scolded Walter, anxiously looking back to his house. The neighbors had just helped the policeman to his feet, and Mr. Brenner was feverishly brushing and rubbing off the mud. Nobody seemed to give any thought to the children. Walter was frantic with impatience.

"They can see us from here," he wailed. "Is there no end to this train?"

Finally, the last of the cars rolled slowly past, and the gates went up. The children leaped across the tracks. Then they stopped and blinked. Mo had disappeared.

"She's gone," gasped Otto. He took off his glasses, polished them with the corner of his jacket, put them on again, and looked down Holle Road.

"She must be hiding," said Gretel. A lock of brown hair tumbled over her nose, and she angrily blew it aside.

"Phew! It's hot," said Erna, holding her hair off the back of her neck. Konrad sat down on the curbstone to take a rest. Only Willy grinned as happily as ever. He was thin and could run a long time without tiring.

Holle Road seemed deserted in the warm afternoon sun.

Far down the county road an empty hay wagon with a two-horse team was pulling out on the way to the fields. The children went on again at a slow pace, searching for Mo in every alleyway, but she was nowhere. They spotted Mr. Aufhauser, the mail carrier, emerging from a house below and ran toward him.

"Hello, Mr. Aufhauser!" called Walter. "Have you seen a girl with a red coat and a red cap?"

"Sure," said Mr. Aufhauser, lighting a long, thin cigar with deliberation.

"Where is she?" shrieked the children.

"My, she was in a hurry," said Mr. Aufhauser, and drew on his cigar with satisfaction. "A while ago she went by me like lightning. 'That won't end well,' I thought. 'She is bound to fall on her face.' She was running down Holle Road, but when Farmer Kuntze pulled out of the court-yard with his team of horses and his hay wagon, she stopped and screamed holy murder. She turned and ran into Church Street. A few small kids ran after her and cried: 'Red cap! Red cap!' Then she ran into the nearest house and slammed the door behind her."

"Which house?" called Walter on the jump.

"I think number 11 or 12," said Mr. Aufhauser. "Now tell me, kids, who is the little girl? I've never seen her around before, and I know every soul in this forsaken place!"

The children took off, leaving Mr. Aufhauser looking after them dumbfounded. They ran into Church Street and stormed into number 10, where Miss Wambacher, the piano teacher, lived. She was just giving a lesson to a little girl who, perched miserably on a piano stool, was practicing scales. When the children crashed in so suddenly, both of them jerked around in fright, and Miss Wambacher said pointedly: "I would be grateful if you would take the trouble to knock!"

"Pardon us, Miss Wambacher," panted Walter, "did you see Mo?"

"What is Mo?" asked the teacher suspiciously.

"Mo is a little girl with a red coat and a red cap," called Gretel.

"Did she want to take piano lessons?" inquired Miss Wambacher in a more friendly tone.

"No," Walter replied, "we're just looking for her."

"There is no such girl here," objected Miss Wambacher. "Now don't bother me any more!"

The children had already disappeared. They entered number 11, next door, where Mr. and Mrs. Grobschmidt were having a late lunch. "Great thunder, have all the children in town gone berserk?" Mr. Grobschmidt shouted, and he pounded the table with his fist. Unfortunately, he hit his soup plate, and the hot soup splashed in his face.

"Pardon us!" stammered Walter. "We are looking for Mo."

"If you devils want to play hide-and-seek, do it outside!" roared Mr. Grobschmidt, and mopped his face with a corner of the tablecloth.

"Is Mo a little girl wearing a red coat?" asked Mrs. Grobschmidt with a smile.

"Oh, yes!" chorused the children, encouraged to have at last found an understanding soul.

"My, what a pretty child she was," continued Mrs. Grobschmidt. "And her eyes! Never saw the like of them before. I said to myself, 'She looks like an angel,' I says. Gus, didn't I say that she looked like an angel?" she asked her husband. But Gus just stared at his soup plate.

"But where is she?" insisted Walter.

"She ran through the house and into the garden," chuckled Mrs. Grobschmidt, who thought it all very amusing. "She tripped over Putzi and fell on her nose. Putzi was lying outside asleep. He whimpered and snapped at her, so she jumped up and hurdled over the fence and was gone. Who is the child? Where is she from?"

"She's from another planet," shrieked Gretel and, before the baffled Grobschmidts caught on, the whole gang ran into the garden. They vaulted over the fence, all at once, so that it nearly collapsed, and Putzi, a small white spitz, yapping and snarling, tried his best to take a chunk out of some leg. Konrad got hung up by his suspenders, and Putzi took a good hold of the seat of his pants and wouldn't let go.

"Help!" Konrad gave out a nerve-shattering howl. Willy and Walter quickly unbuttoned his suspenders and freed him.

"Did he bite you?" sympathized Gretel.

"No," snorted Konrad, and hitched up his suspenders to keep his pants from slipping. Then he felt the seat of his pants and announced, "I've got a hole in my pants. Wait till my father sees it!"

This made the children laugh. They sauntered down the hill and presently reached the market square, where they looked in all directions for Mo. She was nowhere to be seen. On one side of the square rose the majestic old church, and around it, forming a semicircle, were the town hall, the house of the volunteer fire company, and a few stores. In the middle stood the historic St. Matthew's fountain.

"Where could she possibly be?" wondered Walter.

"She surely wouldn't have gone that way, with all the people there," said Otto, and pointed at the Farmers' Market on the other side of the square. There the farmers, who came once a week from the country to sell their produce, had erected long wooden stands under big, gaily colored umbrellas. Eggs, butter and cheese, vegetables and fruits, pastries and flowers, and many other edibles were displayed in profusion. A few of the citizens of Kummersville were gathered around the stands, some to buy, some just to look.

The children walked up to the St. Matthew's fountain and sat down on its stone steps. They were weary and discouraged and did not know what to do next. Konrad stretched out and closed his eyes. His face was purple, and his shirt soaked with perspiration. Gretel leaned against the side of the basin and blinked at the sun. Willy was still looking around searchingly. Erna squatted close to Walter and nervously looked at him out of the corner of her eye.

"Are you very sad that Mo is gone?" she asked.

"Baloney," murmured Walter, and plucked at a few blades of grass sprouting between the stones.

Erna did not know what to say.

It was a beautiful, peaceful summer day. A few fleecy clouds were drifting across the sky, a flock of pigeons circled around the church spire, and a gentle breeze carried

pleasant smells from the direction of the market. It smelled
of herbs, oranges, and salami. A hurdy-gurdy began to grind
out an old folk tune, and a few small girls, with their arms
linked in front of the organ grinder, began to sing:

> *O wee man all alone in the deep dark wood,*
> *He wears upon his head such a queer broad hood.*
> *Tell me quickly if you can*
> *What to call this little man*
> *Who's standing all alone in the deep dark wood.*

"Why doesn't he play something more up-to-date?" Otto
asked disapprovingly.

Two pigeons alighted on the edge of the fountain. First they kept a wary eye on the children, but then they dipped their beaks into the water.

"Mo will never find the Hollewood on her own," fretted Walter.

"Perhaps she still will turn up somewhere," said Gretel, and looked around.

"I know what!" cried Willy. "Let's go into every house and look for her!"

"You're off your rocker!" jeered Erna. "That's impossible." She was still furious because Walter had been short with her.

77

"Chicken!" retorted Willy, and smirked at her defiantly. Erna and Willy were twins, but even so they fought once in a while.

"I'm through with chasing her," Konrad groaned without opening his eyes.

"Those grownups are funny," said Gretel. "Why can't they believe that Mo comes from Asra?"

"Perhaps she really is nuts," muttered Konrad.

"*You* are nuts," cried Gretel, and kicked him.

"Ouch!" yelled Konrad, sitting up.

"If you think Mo is so crazy, you needn't come along," hissed Walter.

"But I want to," replied Konrad.

"Boy, that was something, the way she just snatched the necklace from Klotz!" said Willy, full of admiration.

"Why did they all get so excited over the necklace?" asked Erna.

"It's supposed to be worth a million," said Walter, shrugging his shoulders.

"Is that a lot, a million?" asked Konrad. His grade in arithmetic was always unsatisfactory.

"One million has six zeros," said Otto.

"Boy, that's a lot!" exclaimed Willy.

"If I had a million, I would buy myself a dress of pure silk with no sleeves, like Mo's," sighed Gretel.

"I would buy myself one even prettier than that," declared Erna. She bent over the edge of the fountain and admired her red hair in the reflection of the water. "I would buy one of green velvet."

"Here comes Lottie!" called Walter in surprise.

Lottie came running across the square, her skirt billowing. She was waving both her arms. "Walter! Gretel!" she shouted from afar. "I've got something important to tell you!" With that, she bounced up the steps and stopped breathlessly in front of the children.

Eleven

The Earth Is Full of Tears

"How did you know we were here?" asked Walter.

"I saw you," explained Lottie, and her cheeks glowed with excitement. "Mother sent me up to my bedroom, and when I looked out of the window, I could see you sitting here."

"Did Mother give you permission to leave the house?" Gretel asked sternly.

"No," admitted Lottie with a bad conscience. "I jumped on the roof of the shed and climbed down the ladder because I have something important to tell you."

"They are looking for us, is that it?" Walter asked nervously.

"Oh, no," continued Lottie. "They were quarreling. The policeman wanted them all to go and look for you, but they said they wouldn't do it. They don't know where to look for you, and Father said, 'My children are good children; they surely will bring the little girl back when they realize that the space ship won't come.' That made the sergeant very angry, and he said one couldn't let the little girl run loose with a necklace worth a million. 'That is too dangerous,' he said. 'Somebody could murder her for that.'"

"Murder?" the children shrieked in horror.

"Yes," said Lottie, and nodded fervently.

"Why doesn't the cop look for her himself?" said Walter.

"He isn't able to," replied Lottie, and grinned slyly.

"Why not?" asked Walter.

"His uniform is soaked," said Lottie. "He fell into the puddle, don't you remember, and got it all muddy. Mother had to wash it and then hang it up to dry. Later it has to be pressed. The sergeant had to take everything off, even his pants," she added, blushing.

The children roared with laughter. Willy hopped from one foot to the other and slapped his sides hooting, "His pants. Even his pants! Yahoo!"

When they calmed down, Walter asked Lottie, "Is that why you ran after us?"

"No," said Lottie. "I know where Mo is!"

"What? How? Why? Where?" everybody yelled in confusion.

"In the church," said Lottie proudly.

"In the church?" repeated Walter, completely taken aback.

"Now what makes you think that?" asked Gretel suspiciously. Lottie had a vivid imagination.

"You're sure you're not making this up, Lottie?" Walter asked threateningly.

"Cross my heart," peeped Lottie, rather hurt. "I saw Mo from the window too. She climbed over the fence and ran to the square. She stopped, looking around all the time as though she wanted to hide. Suddenly the church bells rang, and with that she darted into the church."

Walter dashed off; the others followed. In front of the church Walter took off his hat, Otto his cap, and they entered quietly. For a moment they hesitated at the door to allow their eyes to get used to the dark. Someone was playing softly on the organ. After a while, they could distinguish a few old people in the front pews, but there was no sign of Mo. The children walked up the center aisle searching everywhere. Walter even gazed up at the choir loft, but there was only the aged music teacher, Mr. Kronecker, sitting at the organ practicing a choral. Walter knew the choral well, for he often sang in the choir. The grownups insisted that he had a beautiful voice, but he didn't think it so beautiful. The children were just about to leave, dejectedly, when Willy, in a hushed voice, called, "I see her!"

Willy happened to be lynx-eyed. Now the others, too, spied Mo. She was lying in the last pew, nestled in the corner. She had made herself small; one arm was covering her head. She did not stir. The children tiptoed up to her, and Gretel gently touched her arm.

With a start, Mo sat up and looked at the children in a daze. Then, she quickly covered her face with her hands and began to cry. The children, embarrassed, cast their eyes to the floor. After a while Mo only sobbed a bit. She uncovered her face and in surprise looked at her wet fingers.

"My fingers are wet," she whispered.

"You are crying," said Erna.

"But, I have never cried before," said Mo in consternation.

"On earth one cries," said Otto.

"I often cry," said Lottie, about to burst into tears, but she pulled herself together.

"Why did you beat it, Mo?" asked Walter.

"I want to go home," said Mo shyly.

"Alone you could never find the way," said Walter. "We'll take you to your father. We promised you, didn't we?"

Mo looked at him gratefully. "It wasn't nice on Earth without you," she said.

"You were frightened, weren't you?" asked Erna.

Mo nodded. "Very," she admitted.

"Boy!" said Willy. "You sure ran!"

"Two big beasts were coming out of a house," Mo said.

"They had long teeth, and they snorted and wanted to bite me."

The children couldn't help laughing, and an old woman indignantly turned around. "Hush," she called.

The children sheepishly left. Outside, they stood on the steps, squinting in the bright sun after the darkness of the church. It was only then that they discovered that Mo's daintiness had suffered. Her face was smeared from wiping her tears, and her red coat was all dirty, with one pocket half torn off. The seam of her right sleeve had opened, and her knees were scratched.

Gretel wrung her hands. "Goodness, you look awful," she exclaimed with motherly concern.

Mo was embarrassed. "I stepped on a soft animal and fell," she said. "It yelled very much."

The children laughed again. Even Walter joined in the laughter.

"That was Putzi," said Gretel.

"I've got a hole in my pants," said Konrad.

"Why did you run into the church, Mo?" asked Walter.

"The bells rang, so I ran in. Nobody may do me harm in the church, isn't that right?" said Mo.

"But you're wearing the necklace again," Walter observed with alarm.

"It is *my* chain, isn't it?" ask Mo.

"Yes, yes," said Walter, "but you had better give it to me; I will keep it for you until you leave. It's dangerous for you to run around wearing it!"

Mo took off the necklace and handed it to him. Walter immediately buried it in his pants pocket. Then he quickly looked around to see whether anyone had been watching, but there was no one about.

"Why is it dangerous for me to run around with it?" asked Mo.

"Someone might kill you for it," answered Konrad.

"What is that?" asked Mo uneasily.

"To kill means when somebody shoots you or conks you on the head and you're dead," explained Otto. He knew a lot about it from reading his favorite detective stories.

"Oh!" said Mo, her eyes popping. "Nobody conks heads on Asra," she said.

"You're lucky. On earth somebody is killed every day!" cried Willy.

Mo was very frightened. "Will we go at once into the Hollewood?" she asked anxiously.

"First, I must clean you up," Gretel said firmly. "You can't be seen this way. Come!" They walked over to the fountain. Mo had to take off her coat, and Gretel handed it to Erna. "Give it a good shake and turn it inside out," she said busily. "That way nobody will see the torn pocket and the open seam on the sleeve. I need a rag!" She looked at them with impatience.

"I never have rags," grumbled Konrad.

"Do you want me to take my shirt off?" asked Walter helpfully.

"No," said Gretel. "Mother would scold. Do you still have the kerchief?" she asked Mo.

"Oh, yes," said Mo. "I must give it back to my father."

Gretel rinsed it in the fountain and then wiped Mo's face. She kneeled down and scrubbed her knees. Meanwhile,

Erna had shaken the coat and turned it inside out. It was lined with pink silk and looked very pretty even this way. She waited for Mo to put it on again. Mo's blue silk dress had remained clean, although it was somewhat mussed.

Gretel looked up at Mo and said, "Why did you say that these aren't your regular clothes?" She had not forgotten and had wondered all the time why Mo had mentioned that.

"Oh, it was like this . . . " explained Mo with animation. "My father forbade me to wear my Asra clothes on Earth. He said that we might happen to meet humans, and then they would see at once that we came from another planet. Our clothes are quite different from yours."

"Where did you get these clothes," asked Otto dubiously.

Mo broke into laughter, and, as before, it sounded like the melodious note of the lark. She seemed to have overcome the panic that had seized her during her flight through the village.

"I had a little quarrel with my father," she related gleefully. "I did not want to wear the clothes, because they looked so funny. My father once brought them back from Earth. They belong to a big doll in our museum. The doll has a tag and it says on it: 'A little girl from Earth.' We children are fascinated by the doll."

Erna sniffed the coat. "It smells of perfume!"

Mo seemed a bit embarrassed. "It did not smell very pleasant because it had been in the museum for so long," she explained, "so I secretly took a bit of nice-smelling water from my mother and poured it on." She stopped talking and gave the children a guilty look.

"So you're not always such angels either," said Otto with satisfaction.

"We have to go!" urged Walter impatiently.

But Gretel insisted on first combing Mo's hair. To do that, she made Walter give her his pocket comb. Walter happened to have very beautiful, slightly wavy brown hair for which he always carried a pocket comb. Gretel removed Mo's red cap. Walter took it and put it in his pocket. "It's better if Mo doesn't wear it," he explained. "They could spot her too easily."

Gretel tenderly combed Mo's hair; then Erna helped her into the coat. But they were not yet ready; instead they continued to pluck and brush her. They pulled up her socks, smoothed out the pink silk lining, and even retied her shoelaces.

Walter grew angry and shouted: "Now stop all that fuss! We have to start for the Hollewood! The sun will soon go down!"

Reluctantly, Gretel and Erna ceased their efforts to fuss over Mo, and Konrad exclaimed in horror, "Are we going to walk it?"

"Sure," said Walter. "We can't get our bikes and run the risk of getting caught by the police."

"We had better go up Gackenburg Alley by way of the market," suggested Otto. "That way, he's not so likely to see us."

"A good idea," said Walter, and Otto was flattered. But they should never have gone by way of the market place.

Twelve

A Bird on the Butter

Mo was happy to have rejoined the children, and she laughed all the time. But when they passed the old organ-grinder, she stopped and a shadow came over her face. On the organ box sat a little monkey, leashed on a long chain. He was wearing a tiny soldier's uniform, from which his long tail stuck out. In his hands he held a tin cup with which he was begging for coins.

"Is that a little man?" asked Mo, looking frightened.

"No," said Walter, "it's an animal."

"But it has two legs!" said Mo, eying the monkey with suspicion.

"Isn't he cute?" cried out Lottie, and clapped her hands eagerly.

"No," said Mo, vexed. "It is a bad animal."

The children were puzzled.

"Why?" asked Walter.

"It is wearing a uniform," said Mo, and turned her back on the monkey. She was not going to have anything to do with him. Then, in a flash, her gay mood returned, and she laughed. "Oh, we children have those on Asra too!"

On the other side of the square a woman was selling balloons. In one hand she held a bunch of red, green, and blue balloons and in the other an especially big one attached to a string.

Mo ran up to her and snatched the big balloon from her. "Thanks," Mo said.

Walter dashed up in a frenzy. "You have to give the balloon back," he said.

"Why?" Mo asked.

"The balloons belong to her," Walter explained. He quickly returned it to the woman, who nodded amiably.

"But they are only for children," said Mo, confused.

"The woman sells them to children," said Walter. Mo did not seem to understand, but Walter dragged her away and they walked on. Mo turned around a few times to give the balloons a longing look, but then there were many other things to see and she soon forgot about them.

"What is all that?" she asked, pointing to the stands heaped with carrots, cabbages, potatoes, spinach, radishes, tomatoes, turnips, and many other vegetables.

"Those are vegetables," said Gretel, who was following them.

Mo turned and asked, "What does one do with them?"

"People eat them," explained Otto.

"Do they eat them here?" asked Mo, and looked at Walter in amazement.

"No, they eat them at home," said Walter patiently.

Mo again burst into laughter. "Really?" she cried out. "Then why do they first bring them here?" Soon something else caught her attention. "Can one eat *that* too?" she asked, and stood in front of a few baskets filled to the brim with red-cheeked apples. Behind the baskets sat a little old farmer looking rather sullen because he had not yet sold many apples. He had a long nose, and his head was shaven as smooth as an egg. In fact, what hair he had was only some bushy fuzz sprouting from his ears.

"Those are apples," explained Konrad, pushing himself forward. "They taste awfully good." He looked at them longingly. Mo picked up an especially large one and bit into it with zest. The children were horrified.

"You can't do that," Walter whispered.

"Why not?" said Mo, and took another bite. "I'm hungry. I haven't had my pill yet."

"Ten pennies," said the old farmer glumly, and held out his bony hand.

Mo quickly shook the hand. "Are we friends now?" she asked, still chewing.

"The apples are ten pennies apiece," insisted the old man even more sullenly. "They're cheaper if you buy a dozen."

"Are those your apples?" Mo asked hesitatingly.

"Of course," snarled the old man. "Do you think I stole them? Ten pennies," he persisted.

"Do you want to eat them all yourself?" asked Mo in wonderment, and reluctantly took one more bite.

"You bit into the apple; you've got to pay for it," the old man said, and got up.

"She has no money," said Walter.

"What?" fumed the old man. "Where are your parents?" he asked Mo angrily.

"I am alone on Earth," replied Mo, terrified.

Walter took the apple away from her and handed it to the old man.

"Why don't you take it back!" he begged.

"Are you crazy?" asked the old man. "Who would want to buy a bitten apple?"

"Couldn't you cut a piece off?" Gretel asked hopefully.

"No," snapped the old man. "I want ten pennies."

"You are awfully mean," heckled Erna, hiding behind Walter.

"For the love of Pete!" yelled the old man. "If the child has no parents, it shouldn't nibble my apples!"

"My father is on the Moon," explained Mo meekly.

"Where is she from?" the old man shouted at the children.

"From Asra," whimpered Lottie.

"Are you together?" the old man wanted to know.

"Yes," said Walter, "but she's just visiting here."

"Then *you* must pay for the apple!" insisted the old man.

Walter, Willy, Otto, and Konrad desperately searched their pockets, but they knew only too well that they had no money. Willy pulled a small can of earthworms out of his left pocket and from the right one a piece of wood with a long fishing line wound around it, a stump of a candle, two bits of chalk, five playing cards, six fishhooks, several tin soldiers, and finally a small sack of colored marbles. After serious consideration, he offered the marbles to the old man, but the farmer refused them. "I've quit playing with marbles," he growled scornfully.

Konrad dug three caramels out of his pants pocket, gave

them a quick look, and put them back. He obviously could not get himself to part with them. Instead, he tried to interest the old man in the stub of a pencil, but the old man would not even deign to look. "Have you no money?" he asked menacingly.

"No," confessed Walter.

"Don't you get any spending money?" inquired the old man.

"Father has no money to give us," sobbed Lottie.

"Take this for the apple," said Walter, holding up his pocket comb. Nothing could have been more unfortunate, considering that the old farmer did not have a single hair on his head. His face turned purple, and he roared: "Get out of here before I give you a good thrashing! And don't ever let me see you again!"

He did not have to tell the children twice. They fled and kept running until they could no longer see the old man. Only then did they stop to catch their breath.

"That almost did it," panted Walter. He was still clutching the nibbled apple.

"Could I have it now?" begged Konrad.

"Nix," said Walter, and threw the apple away. "It isn't ours."

Willy took off his cap and ran his fingers through his red hair. "Boy, was he a money miser!" he said.

"I would have thrown that apple in his face!" scolded Gretel.

"The apples in our garden are much better," said Erna, wrinkling her nose.

"Why did not that man have any hair?" Mo asked meekly.

"Because he is bald-headed," grumbled Otto scornfully.

"He cried so loud," said Mo.

"You shouldn't have taken the apple," Erna rebuked Mo.

"She doesn't know that one cannot do that," said Walter.

They wanted to walk on when Mo, entranced, stood staring at a wooden cage bursting with live chickens. A farmer's fat wife was dozing beside the cage. "We've got to go!" said Walter, and took Mo by the hand again. But Mo resisted.

"Are those animals too?" she asked excitedly.

"Yes," said Walter, alarmed. "Those are chickens. Come along!"

"Why are they imprisoned?" asked Mo, tears welling up in her eyes.

"So you can't take a bite of them," grinned Willy.

"They kill them and cook them," said Erna.

"I love to eat chicken," said Konrad dreamily.

Suddenly, Mo broke away and ran up to the farmer's fat wife.

"You are a very horrible human!" she shouted at her, and, before the children could stop her, Mo threw back the lid of the cage and, presto, all the chickens fluttered to freedom and ran in all directions, clucking loudly.

At first, the farmer's wife was speechless, but then she jumped up and shrieked: "Help! My chickens! My chickens!" With that, she grabbed Mo by the sleeve and held her. The children were thunderstruck.

Farmers at the nearby stands called: "What's up? What happened?"

"My chickens! My chickens!" howled the farmer's wife. "The brat let my chickens loose!"

A few chickens managed to escape as far as the church; others had taken refuge under the stands and were aimlessly fluttering among the boxes and baskets. The farmers chased them, but they were not so easy to catch. One chicken flew atop a parasol and tipped it over; another fluttered against a flower stand and knocked down all the flowers; while a third, a particularly stupid hen, perched on a large hunk of butter that a farmer had most artistically arranged on his stand. The fellow sprang up as if stung by a wasp and screamed, "Lord Almighty! The dumb bird is sitting on top of my butter!"

The farmer's wife just stood and shrieked without stopping, "My chickens! My chickens! I'll kill that brat!" And she shook Mo violently.

"Please, no!" cried Mo in horror. "You cannot cook me!"

At last Walter sprang into action. He clutched Mo by her free sleeve and tried to pull her away from her captor. But the woman would not let her go, and a tug-of-war followed. Gretel ran up to the woman and shouted in a rage, "Let her go! Let her go! She isn't human; she couldn't help it."

Lottie started to cry and plead, "Please, don't harm her; she comes from Asra!"

The fat wife showed no pity. "Police! Police!" she roared. "My chickens! My chickens!"

As luck would have it, the ripped sleeve, by which she was holding Mo, tore off at that moment, and the children ran away with Mo. They took off helter-skelter, zigzagging their way around the stands, and finally emerged on the square in front of the church. They wanted to run up Church Street, but Willy cried in terror, "Here comes Klotz!"

The policeman came waddling toward the market. He apparently had heard the shouting of the farmer's wife. He obviously was in a rush. His fat stomach bounced up and down like a great rubber ball.

The children turned on their heels and sped into the Gackenburg Alley. They were afraid that the sergeant had seen them and frantically sought a hiding place.

"Quick in here!" cried Walter, and they tumbled head over heels into the small red brick building of the public library. They slammed the door behind them, and Walter, just to make sure, turned the key.

Thirteen

Safety in a Book

The only reason a little place like Kummersville had a public library was that it had been donated by a rich lady from America. She had been born in Kummersville and wanted to give her birthplace a lovely gift.

The librarian's name was Miss Josephine Tim. She was a former schoolteacher for whom the children had great respect. However, they also were fond of her because Miss Tim was always kind to them. She was genuinely pleased whenever the children dropped in to take out books. On those occasions she would have long chats with them—never in a condescending way, like most other grownups, but sensibly and like a friend.

For the moment, the children were much too excited and scared to think of Miss Tim. They stood near the door of the reading room and listened, hearts pounding. Even so, Otto had taken off his cap and Willy his hat, as is proper in a library.

"I hope he didn't see us run in here," whispered Walter. Willy wanted to go to the window and peek out, but Walter warned, "Not you, Willy! They can spot your red hair!" He crept up to the window himself and cautiously looked out.

The street was deserted. Only a lone chicken was running down Gackenburg Alley with a determined air. It probably belonged to the farmer's fat wife. Just then the policeman appeared at the end of the street, walking slowly but surely toward the library. He hesitated every once in a while and looked searchingly in all directions.

"He's coming," Walter announced under his breath and ducked. "He's looking for us!"

The others held their breath without realizing it. Lottie clutched Gretel's skirt for protection, Willy smiled feebly, and Konrad perspired more than ever, only this time from fright. Otto paled and nervously fidgeted with his glasses, while Erna bit her lips.

"Are we going now to the Hollewood?" asked Mo.

"No, not yet," whispered Gretel. "The cop is coming."

"I don't like that bad man in the uniform!" cried Mo in a troubled voice.

"Be quiet!" hissed Erna.

"He's walking by," reported Walter quietly jubilant. "He's turning into Lake Street! Now he has disappeared!"

"Holy Moses!" blurted Otto. "What a break!"

"Yippee, we sure fooled him!" Willy cried triumphantly, rubbing his hands in glee.

"Shall we make a quick getaway?" asked Gretel.

"No," ordered Walter. He stood up and pensively scratched the back of his head. "We'd better stick around until it gets dark. This is the safest place for us."

"But what shall we do here?" sulked Erna.

Walter looked around at the small study where Miss Tim

usually sat. The door was closed. Probably Miss Tim had not noticed that the children were there.

"Let's pretend we're reading," he said.

"Oh, read—!" groaned Konrad peevishly.

"No eats to be had here," grinned Willy.

The children walked up to a long, low table surrounded by small chairs. This was the children's book corner. Directly behind it was a door that led into the garden. The table was piled high with books, picture books and children's magazines. Quickly they all snatched something to read. Otto grabbed *Emil and the Detectives,* Willy *The Pathfinder,* and Walter *Quo Vadis.* Gretel wavered between *My Friend Flicka* and *Heidi* and finally chose *Heidi.* Lottie

was delighted to find *The Prince and the Pauper*, her favorite book, and Erna chose a magazine with the latest doll fashions and began to study them carefully. Konrad fumbled among the books without being able to make up his mind until he accidentally came upon the fairy tale *Never Never Land*, which completely enthralled him because of the pictures of roast pigeons flying into people's mouths. Mo had not taken a book. She was completely fascinated by the doings of the others.

"Are we going to the Hollewood now?" she asked.

"We have to wait until it gets dark," said Walter.

"When does it get dark on Earth?" she asked.

"When the sun goes down," replied Otto.

"When does the Sun go down?" asked Mo.

"When evening comes," Willy told her.

"It won't be long now," consoled Walter. "You, too, must pick up a book!"

"What is a book?" asked Mo.

"Books are to read," said Otto.

"We don't have books," said Mo.

"But don't you read?" Gretel asked in astonishment.

"We have little machines into which we look and read," explained Mo.

"Oh, boy, do you crank them?" Willy wanted to know.

"How pretty!" called Mo. A small globe rested on the table. "That is the way Asra looks when we visit our artificial moon."

"That is the earth," informed Otto. "We live here!" He tapped his finger on a small spot on the globe.

"Mo, perhaps you'd better stop telling people that you're from Asra," said Walter. "Otherwise we might never get to the Hollewood."

"Are all big people bad?" asked Mo.

"The cop thinks you're crazy and wants to lock you up," said Erna.

"What is crazy?" inquired Mo, looking worried.

"Crazy is when you roll your eyes and run through the streets with no clothes on," declared Otto.

"Oh," said Mo, frightened. "I do not do that!"

The children laughed. Gretel pushed *Heidi* into Mo's hand and said, "Try it."

Mo looked at a loss. "I can only speak your language; I cannot read it," she admitted.

"That's all right," said Walter. "When Miss Tim comes, she must think that you, too, are reading."

Obediently, Mo stared at the pages, and the others picked up their books again, but they were nervous and hungry and could not concentrate. Even Erna had lost interest in her doll dresses. She dropped the magazine and looked at Mo. "Why did you let the chickens escape?" she asked accusingly.

"They looked so sad," said Mo softly.

"Chickens always look sad," grumbled Konrad.

"Chickens cost a lot," said Walter with concern. "I hope they didn't all run away."

"We have chicken every Sunday," said Erna.

"You're lying," chuckled Willy. "Last Sunday we had pot roast."

"*You* are lying!" said Erna indignantly.

"We have roast goose every Sunday," said Konrad devoutly.

"We have Bratwurst," Lottie admitted blushingly.

"I like that too," said Konrad benignly.

Suddenly all the children jumped to their feet, and Mo rose with them. "Is it now that we go to the Hollewood?" she said happily. But the only reason they had risen was because Miss Tim had entered the room.

Fourteen

Kri Is a Pretty Name

Miss Tim had white hair, but, despite it, she did not look at all old. She wore large horn-rimmed spectacles, behind which soft brown eyes looked amiably at the world. She came out of her study carrying a pile of books, which she put on a shelf. Only then did she discover the children.

"Hello, children," she said with a note of surprise.

"How are you, Miss Tim!" chorused the children.

"How nice that you have come to read!" said Miss Tim appreciatively. She took off her glasses and glanced out of the window. "Wouldn't you rather be playing outdoors? It is such a lovely day, after all."

"We—we've been playing all day," said Walter, choking with embarrassment.

"Keep your seats, please," said Miss Tim, and came closer. "It's hard to read standing up, isn't it?"

The children sat down and took up their books. Mo dutifully glanced into hers.

"I really should put you out," Miss Tim said teasingly. "It's almost six; I usually close the library at this time."

"Six?" stammered Walter. He was horrified that Miss Tim

might turn them away from their safe hiding place. "Couldn't we stay until it gets dark?" He hesitated.

"Have you had your supper?" asked Miss Tim.

"No," groaned Konrad.

"Are you so anxious to read that you are even willing to go without food?" laughed Miss Tim.

"No," said Konrad.

"We are too!" Walter added quickly.

"Why don't you simply take the books home with you?" suggested Miss Tim.

"We—we—we're having general house-cleaning," said Walter, blushing. That was a silly excuse, but he could not think of anything better at the moment. He did not dare to explain to Miss Tim why they were hiding in the library.

Miss Tim laughed good-humoredly. "Very well," she said. "If you're so anxious to read, I'll just have to close up later tonight. I still have to tidy up my study anyway. Besides, I should write a letter to Miss Kunkel. She still hasn't returned *A Lady of Fashion*. Then you must go, children. I'll have to go home to feed my cats and water my flowers. And if I don't cover up my canary's cage, he will not be able to sleep. You can understand that, can't you?"

"Yes," chorused the children.

Curious to see what he was reading, she stepped behind Walter and looked over his shoulder. "What are you reading?" she asked with interest.

Walter stood up and gave her his book. "*Quo Vadis*, Miss Tim," he said.

"Now where did I leave my glasses!" Miss Tim asked.

"You have them in your hands," Walter said politely.

"Oh yes, dear me," said Miss Tim. "I'm getting more and more befuddled in my old days!" She laughed at herself and returned the book to Walter. "Do you like it?" she asked.

"Yes, Miss Tim," said Walter.

"Well, I mustn't keep you from your reading any longer," said Miss Tim.

Walter sat down again. Miss Tim was about to leave when, as bad luck would have it, she noticed Mo.

"But you aren't reading at all, my child," she said with a smile.

Frightened, Mo looked at Miss Tim with her big violet-blue eyes. "I read well," she said uncertainly.

"But you're holding the book upside down!" exclaimed Miss Tim, chuckling.

Hastily, Mo turned her book sideways, but that way she could not have read either.

Miss Tim was really most astonished. "Don't you know how to read?" she asked.

"Oh, yes," said Mo. "We have no books."

Miss Tim was perplexed and leaned against the edge of the table.

"You don't have books?" she said slowly. "Who has no books?"

"We," said Mo reluctantly.

"Is that so?" said Miss Tim. "Just what do you read, if you have no books?" she asked, amused.

"We have little machines; we look into them," explained Mo softly.

By now the children were nervously watching Miss Tim and Mo from behind their books. Miss Tim laughed. "But you probably love to read fairy tales, don't you, child?" she asked.

Mo grew more confident. She seemed to take a liking to Miss Tim. "We have many fairy tales," she said, nodding with animation. "I like most the one about the child from Earth who comes to Asra and does not care for pills. It has lovely pictures. They are full of colors and glow, and everything looks alive, just as in reality," she confided happily.

"I don't know that fairy tale," said Miss Tim. "Did you invent it yourself?"

"Oh, no," protested Mo. "I would not know how to. It is known to all children on Asra."

"Asra is a fairy land, is it?" asked Miss Tim.

Mo shrieked with laughter. "Asra, that is we!" she exclaimed, but then she noticed that Walter was giving her frantic looks, and she stopped.

"My child, you're all at sixes and sevens!" Miss Tim exclaimed. "You're wearing your coat inside out!"

"I fell, because something yelled," said Mo.

"And why do you have only one sleeve?" asked Miss Tim, shaking her head. Indeed, Mo did look a bit funny, with her right arm hanging bare out of the coat.

"The fat Earth woman has my sleeve," she said scornfully. Miss Tim looked at the children in astonishment.

"What does this mean, children?" she asked.

However, the children had their noses buried in their books. Only their unruly hair could be seen.

"Why does the fat earth woman have your sleeve?" Miss Tim at last asked Mo.

"Because I let the animals free," Mo said cautiously.

"Animals? What kind of animals?" asked Miss Tim.

"They have two legs, no arms, and a pointed nose," said Mo.

"Tell me, aren't you in school yet?" asked Miss Tim.

"Oh, yes," said Mo. "All children must go to school!"

"But you don't go to school here in Kummersville, do you?" inquired Miss Tim. "I've never seen you before."

"I have never seen you before either," said Mo. "Your hair is all white."

"When one grows old, one's hair turns gray," said Miss Tim, smiling.

"Are you already a thousand years old?" asked Mo.

"No, I am not that old," said Miss Tim. "Nor am I likely to get that old."

"That is bad!" said Mo with concern.

"Incidentally, where are you from, my child?" asked Miss Tim.

"I am not supposed to tell anybody any more," murmured Mo with a furtive side glance.

"Why not?" asked Miss Tim.

"If I do, we'll never get to the Hollewood," breathed Mo faintly.

For a moment Miss Tim was speechless. "What is your name, child?" she asked.

"May I tell?" asked Mo, looking at Walter.

"Her name is Mo," rasped Walter from behind his book.

"Mo is a pretty name," said Miss Tim, and nodded at her with a friendly smile.

"Isn't it?" said Mo cheerfully. "My father wanted to call me Kri, but I don't like Kri."

"Kri is also quite pretty," said Miss Tim. "You come from a foreign land, don't you? You have a curious accent."

"Normally I speak differently," said Mo.

"And where do your parents live?" asked Miss Tim.

"In a house," responded Mo.

"In what country?" asked Miss Tim patiently.

"I don't know what a country is," said Mo.

"How long have you been going to school, Mo?" asked Miss Tim.

"We children all go to school when we are fifty years old," said Mo.

"My, you are a crazy child," laughed Miss Tim.

"No," cried Mo in horror and, quick as a wink, crept under the table.

The children were frightened, but Miss Tim was even more so. "Heavens! What is the matter with the child?" she asked.

"She . . . she is very timid," stammered Walter.

Miss Tim got on her knees, peered under the table, and called: "Mo, why did you creep under the table?"

"Do not lock me up, please not!" cried Mo.

"Who wants to lock you up?" said Miss Tim.

"Please, I am not crazy!" cried Mo.

"But I was only joking," answered Miss Tim, quite confused. "You mustn't take offense so quickly!"

"Humans are bad. I want to go home," sobbed Mo.

Miss Tim now joined Mo under the table and tried to calm her. "But, child, I didn't really mean it when I said you were crazy," she said.

"I am not crazy," shrieked Mo. "I never roll my eyes."

"Now, come," said Miss Tim, almost pleading. "Be sensible. I promise you, nobody will lock you up!"

"The bad man in the uniform promised that too, but he broke his promise," cried Mo. "He did not want to give the chain back to me."

The children stared, not knowing what to do. Finally, Gretel joined Mo and Miss Tim under the table and said: "Mo, Miss Tim is a good human."

Walter called: "Mo, I swear Miss Tim won't harm you. You do trust *me*, don't you, Mo?"

"Do we now go to the Hollewood?" called Mo from below.

"Later we will certainly go to the Hollewood," answered Walter. "I'll see to it that nobody will lock you up. And Miss Tim won't lock you up either. Miss Tim is a schoolteacher."

"Oh," said Mo, and crept from under the table.

She looked at Miss Tim with respect. "At home nobody is ever locked up," she said, wiping away her tears.

Gretel reappeared, and Miss Tim got up groaning and dusted off her skirt. "You really gave me a scare, child!" she reproached Mo, and drew a sigh of relief.

"Now tell me, children," she said. "What is the matter with the little girl? Why is she so scared? How do you know her? And why is her talk so odd?"

"She is . . . she has . . . she comes . . ." Walter began to stammer, but at that moment someone shook the front door with determination and then banged against it in a rage.

"But why is the door locked?" said Miss Tim in consternation.

"That must have happened by mistake," Walter managed to mumble.

The banging became more and more furious, and Miss Tim walked over and asked, "Who's there?"

"The police!" sounded Sergeant Klotz's bass voice.

"The police?" called Miss Tim in utter surprise. "Is that you, Klotz?"

"Yes!" came the roar of Klotz. "Chief sergeant Klotz!"

"And what do you want?" asked Miss Tim.

"Open up, please!" called the sergeant.

"It's almost closing time," said Miss Tim loudly. "Why don't you come for your books tomorrow, please!"

"I don't read books!" roared the officer. "Open up in the name of the law!"

"Well, now I'm really curious," said Miss Tim, and unlocked the door.

"Where are the children?" called the sergeant, as he came bursting in.

"What children?" asked Miss Tim.

"Walter Brenner and his sisters. And a little girl with blonde hair and a red coat and a diamond chain around her neck!" shouted the policeman excitedly.

"Goodness, gracious!" exclaimed Miss Tim. "What do you want with those children? There they sit, reading!" She turned around and gaped. The children were no longer there. The door to the garden stood wide open.

Fifteen

Everything Scratches, Everything Pricks

As soon as the children heard the sergeant's voice, they took off through the garden door. They ran up a narrow, winding lane and came out on Lake Street. Here, at the edge of the town, were the open fields. The children ran across a potato field toward the county road. But just before they got to it, they saw some trucks driving out from Kummersville. They quickly jumped into the road ditch and crouched low so as not to be seen.

"Those are the farmers from the market," said Otto, pointing. "They are going home now."

"Perhaps the farmer's fat wife is among them," said Gretel.

"And the nasty codger with his apples," added Erna.

They waited in the ditch until they heard the last truck pass by. Then Walter crept up the bank and looked around. "Stay where you are! More are coming!" he called out, sliding back into the ditch.

The others were quite content to have a moment's rest. "The county road isn't safe," worried Walter. "We have to figure out another way to get to the Easter path."

"We could take the trail leading back of the Kummer-hill," suggested Otto.

"Not on your life!" groaned Konrad. "Nothing but steep ups and downs that way!"

"That's it," said Walter. "We're sure not to be seen there; nobody ever uses it."

"But what about Lottie?" asked Gretel. "We can't take her into the forest so late in the evening."

"Konrad will take her home," ordered Walter.

"I'm not a baby nurse!" objected Konrad.

"I don't want to go home," Lottie immediately began to wail. "If I come home alone, I'll be spanked. Please, please, I want to see the space ship too!"

"Why does she cry?" asked Mo feelingly.

"She doesn't want to go home," said Gretel.

"Is she not allowed to come with us?" asked Mo.

"She's too little," said Walter.

"But she has fast legs," Mo pointed out.

"It's beginning to get dark, and our parents will worry," explained Walter.

"But I've often been with you in the forest in the evening," sobbed Lottie. "Daddy and Mummy know that you look after me!"

Gretel hugged her and dried her tears. "We might be out much too late tonight," she said. "Be a good girl, Lottie, and go home."

"Erna can take her home," said Willy with a grin.

"Are you crazy!" shouted Erna. "Why don't *you* take her home? The cop might catch me and lock me up and ask me where you are. What should I tell him?"

"Tell him we're on Asra," suggested Willy.

"That fellow Klotz might do anything," said Otto.

"Supposing he locked up Lottie!" said Gretel with alarm.

"Perhaps we had better take her along, after all," suggested Walter, softening.

"And don't forget, I told you where to find Mo," piped Lottie, eying Walter anxiously.

"You certainly did us a great service," said Walter soothingly. Lottie beamed.

"But you mustn't get tired," Gretel warned her.

"Oh, great!" cried Lottie jubilantly. "I'm not a bit tired, not the least bit. I certainly won't get tired either."

Mo was happy too. "I like Lottie," she said. "She is very pretty."

"Do you like us too?" Gretel asked anxiously.

"I like all of you," blushed Mo.

"Do you think I'm pretty too?" Erna asked tensely.

"You have many little spots on your face," said Mo.

Erna was embarrassed. "Those are freckles," she explained. "Mummy said they will disappear when I am grown up."

"Your nose is very nice," said Mo, "and you also have beautiful hair. It looks like the setting Sun."

"Really?" gushed Erna. But then she sighed and added: "Oh, you just say that. I wish I were as beautiful as you are."

"But what shall we do when we return home without Mo and the necklace?" asked Otto. The thought of the sergeant was still worrying him. "Nobody will believe us when we say that she flew back to Asra."

"When she's gone, she's gone," Walter said gruffly. "I don't care what happens after that."

"But I do!" Otto objected angrily.

"Coward!" taunted Walter.

That made Otto even more angry. "The sergeant might think that we killed Mo and stole her necklace," he said.

"You're nuts," said Walter. "Let Klotz look for Mo until he's blue in the face. If he can't find her, it isn't our fault."

"Poppycock," shouted Otto. "We'll be arrested and spend the rest of our lives in jail, just because Mo hasn't been found."

"Boy," declared Willy, "that would be terrific! I've always wanted to be in a jail!"

"You're all off your rockers!" said Walter. "We're innocent, aren't we? Nobody is allowed to lock us up." But he wasn't so sure. "Can your father write our language?" he asked Mo thoughtfully.

"My father can do anything," said Mo, nodding eagerly.

"Your father must give us an excuse in writing saying that you flew back to Asra with him," said Walter.

"And that you took the necklace with you!" interjected Otto.

"What is an excuse?" inquired Mo.

"An excuse is when you didn't go to school and your mother gives you a letter for the teacher to say that you've been sick," explained Otto.

"We are never sick," said Mo, "and we always go to school."

"If we can't prove that you flew back to Asra, the bad

man with the uniform will lock all of us up," Gretel tried to explain.

"Just like the chickens?" asked Mo, startled.

"Yes," said Walter, trying to impress on her the urgency of the matter.

"I will tell my father," Mo said hastily. "And I will tell him that you are good humans. Then he will surely give you an excuse."

That eased their minds, and they thanked her.

On the horizon the sun was disappearing behind the range of the distant Holle Mountains sparkling in the bluish dusk. The sky was cloudless. A few saucy swallows swooped down close over the heads of the children. Somewhere from a barnyard sounded the barking of a dog, the plaintive mooing of cows waiting to be milked.

"The Sun is going down," Mo observed in astonishment.

"Doesn't the sun set on Asra?" Willy asked eagerly.

"Oh, yes," said Mo, "but it takes much, much longer. Here it sets so quickly."

"On earth everything happens in a jiffy," said Otto.

"We must get going!" ordered Walter, climbing the slope to see whether all was clear. "They're all gone," he reported. "Let's go."

The children crossed the county road and jumped down the embankment. They beat their way through some underbrush and reached the Hollebrook.

"Must we always run?" complained Mo, out of breath.

"We mustn't be seen," said Walter, "or they'll be after us."

"The Earth is very exhausting," sighed Mo.

Beyond, the children could see the slope of the Kummer-hill, but first they had to walk to a small footbridge in order to cross the brook, still swollen by the rain of the morning. Then they crawled up the slope like monkeys. On the other side of the hill, the boys simply slid down on the seats of their pants while the girls clambered down backwards. Lottie was always in the lead. She tried her best not to drop behind for fear that Walter might send her home. At last, only a thick hedge of wild raspberries separated them from the footpath, but the sharp thorns slowed their progress, and they had to be very careful not to hurt themselves.

"Everything scratches, everything pricks," complained Mo scornfully. Her right arm, which was bare, had, in fact, been sorely scratched, and she looked at it sadly. Walter helped her as much as he could, but finally the silk lining of her coat caught on the thorny twigs and she was stuck.

"Slip off your coat, but be careful," Walter advised her. Mo did and got free. With a quick jerk, Walter pulled the coat loose, but not without tearing the silk lining to shreds. He wrapped the coat around his arms and cleared a path for Mo. The others were waiting impatiently on the footpath. Only Konrad no longer seemed to be in a hurry. He stuffed his mouth full of raspberries and kept picking more.

Mo put on her coat. "Why do those little trees prick so?" she asked.

"Why, don't you have thorns?" asked Gretel. "Don't you have climbing roses too?"

"Our flowers have nothing sharp," said Mo.

"You people have nothing that bites, nothing that pricks. It sounds kind of dull," observed Otto.

"You have bloody scratches on your arm, Mo!" said Gretel. "Does it hurt?"

"A bit," said Mo.

"Perhaps your head is better now," said Gretel. "I could tape that bandage to your arm." She carefully peeked under the bandage and said, "The bruise is better already." She gently pulled the bandage off and applied it to the worst scratch on Mo's arm. "There, it doesn't hurt any more, does it?" she asked.

"No," said Mo stoutly.

Now the children did not have to run any longer. The footpath was well hidden, and there was no one to be seen anywhere. As it was, they could not have run. The ups and downs were steep, just as Konrad had said, and to make matters worse, they often had to climb over rocks and crawl under low branches. Even so, they reached the Hollewood in better time than they had expected because the footpath was so much shorter than the county road. One more slope and they could see the edge of the forest a short distance off.

"We've almost made it!" Walter called cheerfully.

Willy waved his hat in the air and shouted, "Yippee!" With that, he lost his balance and tumbled down the hill like an avalanche. When he reached the bottom, he remained motionless.

"Willy!" yelled Erna in horror, and heedlessly lunged down the steep slope after him. The others followed as quickly as they could. Erna grabbed Willy by the hair and lifted his head.

"Are you alive?" she cried, terrified.

Willy screwed up his face in a grimace, which made all his freckles melt into one big blotch. He murmured, "Boy, what fun to roll downhill!" But it could not have been too much fun, for his nose was bleeding and his face was scraped.

"Your nose is bleeding," Erna said reproachfully.

Willy sat up without paying any attention to his nose. Instead, he sadly looked at his hat. During his forced descent he had held onto it for dear life, but it was badly crushed and the feather was gone.

"What a lousy break," he complained. "My beautiful hat!" He was very fond of it.

"Lie flat on your back and your nose will stop bleeding," said Walter.

Willy flattened out again, stretched his arms and legs, and kept still.

This worried Mo. She knelt down beside him and caressed him timidly.

"Are you sick?" she asked with concern.

"I'm no chick," murmured Willy.

"What is a chick," asked Mo.

"A chick is a baby chicken," said Gretel.

That made Mo laugh. "No, you are not a baby chicken," she said to Willy. "You are a baby man."

Suddenly Willy jumped up and squirmed like a madman.

"Ouch! Ouch! Ouch!" he yelled, trying to tear the shirt off his back.

"What is it?" the children cried in alarm.

"I was lying on an anthill!" shouted Willy. "Quick, help me! Ouch, ouch!"

"Take off your pants," shrieked Erna.

"Not the pants!" yelled Willy. "They've crawled down my back!"

Walter grabbed Willy's shirt, wanting to pull it over his head, but it was not unbuttoned and Willy almost suffocated. Fortunately, all the buttons popped and off came the shirt. Willy shook it out and then inspected it inch by inch, flicking off the ants. "Boy, they sure can bite," he groaned.

"We must push on," warned Walter.

Willy put his shirt on, rubbed his nose, and grinned.

"Now we're not in such a hurry any more, are we?"

sighed Gretel. She was a bit tired. "Over there is the Holle-wood, and the stars haven't even come out yet."

"We still have to find the Easter path," cautioned Walter.

"It can't be far," said Otto hopefully. But his optimism proved wrong.

Sixteen

The Swamp Is for Adults Only

First, they had to wake Konrad. He had curled up in a
sand ditch and fallen fast asleep.

Walter shook him. "Konrad, we have to be on our way!"
he called.

Konrad shot up and looked around in a daze. "Breakfast
ready?" he mumbled.

The others laughed, and he felt embarrassed. "I'm dying
of hunger," he murmured.

"Give your belt another hitch. We haven't eaten either,"
said Walter. "You can make up for it after you get home."

"They'll all be through by that time," groaned Konrad.

There was only one more hill they had to climb, but
behind it the footpath came to an abrupt end. They faced
a swamp with a thick growth of swamp grass. It extended
as far as the eye could reach along both sides of the Hollewood.

"Jeepers, I think that's the Cambeck Swamp," said Walter, taken aback.

"Do we have to go through it?" Erna asked nervously.

"If I only knew how!" replied Walter.

"Perhaps we had better go back to the county road," Otto suggested.

"Not me," Konrad objected, and defiantly sat down on the ground.

"What fun to walk through the tall grass," said Willy. His nose had stopped bleeding, and he was ready to tackle anything again.

"That's frightfully dangerous!" warned Erna.

"Just a bit slippery," said Willy.

Walter hesitated. He knew the swamp was dangerous, but to return to the county road and make a fresh start for the Hollewood would take too much time. It would soon be dark. "The footpath ends here; that must mean something," he said musingly.

"It means that here the world is nailed up with boards," observed Otto.

"Give him a chance to think!" Gretel snarled at him. She had complete confidence in her brother.

Suddenly it came to Walter. "Now I remember," he said. "The old shepherd, Paul, once told me how to cross the Cambeck Swamp. From where the footpath ends, we walk straight toward a marker at the edge of the forest. That way nothing can happen. It's only a bit damp, and one must watch out for the holes."

"I don't see any marker," grumbled Otto. The swamp grass was so tall that the children couldn't see above it. They could not even make out the tops of the trees beyond it.

Walter ran a little way up the slope and looked across to the forest.

"I see the marker," he shouted.

"Where?" the others chorused, running up.

Only Konrad remained sitting. As long as there was nothing to eat, he didn't care what happened.

"Do you see the tall birch tree among the spruce?" asked Walter. "It has a red spot painted on it. That's the marker."

"Are you sure?" asked Otto doubtingly.

"What else could it be?" insisted Walter.

"Well, O.K.," Otto reluctantly agreed. "I just don't feel like drowning."

"But you know how to swim!" snapped Gretel.

"Ha ha ha! Swim in the swamp!" snickered Otto. "It would gobble you up like a cat does a mouse, and you'd never be seen again!"

Gretel and Erna were rather scared, but Walter and Willy were not so easily intimidated. They ran back to the swamp, and Gretel, Erna, and Otto followed with mixed feelings.

"If you're afraid, Willy and I will go on alone with Mo," said Walter. "I'm sure that is the marker."

"All right, I'll come," said Otto, "but if you can't see the marker, how do you expect to walk toward it?"

They had returned to the tall swamp grass and no longer could see the red spot on the birch tree.

"How stupid," grumbled Walter. "The grass is too tall, or maybe we're too short!"

"This swamp is for adults only," jeered Otto.

"If only we knew how to fly now," remarked Willy.

"We children on Asra all know how to fly," Mo said quietly. She was tired and had to force herself to keep her eyes open. Lottie was tired too, but she would rather have bitten off her tongue than admit it.

"Let's go back to the road," said Otto.

Walter ignored him. Lost in thought, he was staring at Lottie. She immediately became suspicious and hid behind Gretel.

"I don't want to go home," she whimpered.

"Lottie is our solution!" he said cheerfully.

"How so?" the others asked, dumbfounded.

"Lottie doesn't weigh much," said Walter. "I think I can manage to carry her on my shoulders." The others did not understand what he had in mind.

"Come here, Lottie," Walter beckoned smilingly.

But Lottie did not quite trust him. "You . . . you said I could come along," she sobbed.

"And what luck that you did come with us," said Walter. "If it weren't for you, Mo would never get back to Asra."

"Really?" called Lottie proudly and rushed up to him. Walter lifted her on his shoulders and walked into the tall grass. He was completely engulfed by it, but Lottie's head stuck out above the top. They heard him ask her, "Can you see the red spot on the birch, Lottie?"

"Yes!" cried Lottie.

Now the children understood why Lottie could help them, and they clapped their hands in glee.

"Hurrah!" shouted Willy.

"Walter is sharp," said Erna.

Walter was flattered, and he laughed as he returned with Lottie. But he soon became serious.

"Now listen," he warned them. "You have to follow close behind me. Single file! And don't fall back, even for a moment! First comes Mo. Then you, Gretel. Don't take your eyes off Mo and see that she doesn't get off the trail. The rest of you must be very careful to keep up with the one ahead of you. And you, Lottie, you keep your eyes glued to the red spot! Don't look around! You will guide me by my ears as though we were playing horsie!"

"Oh, good!" cried Lottie.

"You must steer me in a straight line toward the red marker," continued Walter. "If I veer to the left, you must pull my right ear, and if I veer to the right, you pull my left ear! Do you know right from left?"

"Right is this side," called out Lottie.

"Ouch!" winced Walter. She had given his right ear a hefty tug. "You don't have to pull quite so hard."

"And left is this side," said Lottie, pulling his left ear, this time a bit more gently.

Walter was satisfied, but once more he warned her: "Lottie, you've got to do a good job. Our lives depend on you. Do you understand?"

"Yes," said Lottie, very flattered.

"Well, let's go then," Walter called out, and, with Lottie astride his shoulders, disappeared in the swamp grass. The others followed in single file, close together, as they had been ordered.

First came Mo, then Gretel, and then the rest. Otto, as usual, brought up the rear. The ground was wet and slippery, and they sank in mud up to their ankles.

"Eeks! My pretty shoes are getting all wet," complained Erna.

"Never mind!" called Walter. "You can never tell what you might step on. Better keep them on! Take care you don't trip!"

Locusts chirped, grasshoppers chattered, and suddenly, as if by signal, thousands of frogs began their evening serenade.

"Who cries so loud?" Mo asked fearfully.

"They are frogs," called Gretel. "They are harmless."

"They are good frogs!" shouted Otto.

"Boy, we are going great guns," Willy observed happily.

"Help!" Erna shrieked.

"What's the matter?" called Walter, and stopped in his tracks.

"Help!" Erna howled again. She had fallen into a hole up to her waist. "Rescue me!" she wailed.

Quickly Willy and Konrad grabbed her and pulled her out. There was a "pop" as though a cork had been pulled out of a bottle. Then they were on firm ground again.

"Ugh, horrible!" she exclaimed with a shudder. "I'm all wet!"

"What happened?" called Walter, who could not see through the tall grass.

"A frog leaped at me and wanted to bite me!" yelled Erna. "I was so scared that I fell into a hole."

The others laughed, relieved that she was all right.

"Frogs don't bite, you sissy," said Willy.

"I can't stand frogs!" Erna called angrily. She was quite miserable, soaked to the waist.

"You'll stay in line, even if a crocodile leaps at you!" scolded Walter, and plodded on.

The others roared with laughter but were doubly careful not to fall into a hole themselves.

"The forest! I can see the forest!" Lottie cried out jubilantly. A moment later Walter stepped onto firm ground and called happily, "Come on, come on! Here we are!"

Mo, who had held onto his suspenders, also was clear of the swamp, and then Gretel, Willy, Erna, and Konrad appeared in quick succession. Ahead of them was a small, dry field and beyond it, finally, the Hollewood.

Walter lifted Lottie off his back, stretched and straightened himself, and mopped his brow. "We did all right," he said, taking a deep breath.

Mo sat down in the grass and woefully inspected her pretty velvet slippers and her socks, which were wet and dirty. But Erna was much worse off. Her skirt was dripping, and everything under it was soaked too.

"What shall I do?" she whimpered.

"Nothing," said Walter. "It will dry by itself."

The children sat down, took off their shoes and socks, and wrung them out as best they could. Then they pulled out some grass and tried to dry their feet with it. This didn't help much, so they simply put their wet shoes and socks back on. Gretel was thankful that she was wearing her old sandals and no stockings.

In a few minutes, Walter discovered that Otto was missing. "Where is Otto?" he called, and jumped up with a start.

"He was close behind me," said Konrad.

"Otto!" Walter shouted with such force that his face grew red.

"Otto! Otto!" howled the others in chorus.

They listened anxiously, but there was only the croaking of the frogs and the hoarse call of three crows swooping across the swamp.

Otto did not answer.

Seventeen

When You're Dead, You're Not Supposed to Yell

Walter turned pale. "Otto, Otto, where are you?" he shouted again.

"I'm sure he drowned," wailed Erna, covering her face with her hands.

"No! No!" Gretel wanted to run back into the swamp, but Walter held her back. "Are you crazy?" he shouted. "You stay here. I'll look for Otto." He dove head-first into the high grass just as Otto was emerging, and their heads collided with a bang.

"Ouch!" Their voices sounded in unison.

"Where were you?" snapped Walter, rubbing his forehead on which a great bump was beginning to swell. But he was delighted that Otto was safe.

"I had a terrible experience," said Otto hoarsely.

"What happened?" the others asked excitedly, and gathered around him.

"Tell, tell!" Willy called eagerly.

Otto's knees were a bit shaky, and he had to sit down. Then he began. "I had stopped to wipe off my glasses . . ."

"Always those glasses!" Walter interrupted, shaking his head. "Some day they'll be the death of you!"

"When they are dirty, I have to clean them so I can see," Otto objected, feeling hurt.

"But that couldn't have been so terrible?" exclaimed Konrad.

"Dope!" said Otto. "*That* wasn't so terrible, but I was just putting my glasses back on when a huge snake came rushing toward me out of the swamp . . ."

"A snake!" Erna shrieked with a shudder.

"Yes," continued Otto. "It opened its mouth and stuck out its tongue."

"Jeepers!" groaned Gretel.

"What did you do?" asked Willy.

"I played dead," said Otto. "I couldn't run away in the swamp."

"Why didn't you call for help?" asked Konrad.

"When you're dead, you're not supposed to yell," said Otto.

"Was it a copperhead?" asked Willy, completely entranced.

"How could I tell without my glasses," replied Otto.

"Did it bite you?" Walter asked anxiously.

"No," said Otto. "I didn't stir, so it moved off and so did I."

"You were lucky to have found the way!" said Walter.

"I saw your tracks," Otto replied smugly.

"Poor Otto!" said Gretel. Her hair was hanging over her face, and by now it had become so straggly that she could not control it.

"We really thought you were dead," said Willy.

Mo, who was sitting in the grass, had listened with interest.

"What is a copperhead?" she wanted to know.

"A copperhead is a long, sleek animal without legs," said Walter. "If it bites you, it makes you very sick."

"Why?" asked Mo.

"It's poisonous," said Gretel.

"What is poisonous?" asked Mo.

"Poisonous is worse than biting," said Otto.

"Why does the animal do it?" asked Mo, and frowned.

"It's a very, very bad animal," said Gretel.

"Because it has no legs?" asked Mo.

"No, not because of that," said Walter. "It can run very well."

"One cannot run without legs," said Mo.

"Sure one can!" called Willy. "Look, I'll show you!" He stretched out in the grass and wiggled like a snake.

"That does not make you go very fast," Mo said disapprovingly.

"That's because I'm not a real snake," said Willy, discouraged.

Walter looked up at the sky. "We can take a little rest," he said. "The stars haven't come out yet." The truth was that he, too, was tired, and he felt like stretching out awhile. He threw himself on the soft ground, pulled out a blade of grass, and began to chew it. Then he folded his arms under his head and watched a hawk circling high above.

The others followed his example and settled down. The

field in which they lay was really most inviting. Bluebells grew everywhere. An occasional butterfly fluttered about, and from the forest came the twitter of birds. A cool breeze descended from the mountains to the south, sending soft ripples over the swamp grass. There was a rustling in the treetops and the smell of pine needles and sweet clover. Mo put her head in her hands and gazed off as if lost in dreams. To her, the Earth seemed pleasant again. Suddenly, she sat up and laughed merrily. "There sits a baby chicken!" she exclaimed. At the edge of the forest a finch, perched on a branch, was twittering to his heart's content.

"That's no baby chicken; that's a finch," said Gretel.

"What is a finch?" asked Mo.

Walter spat out his blade of grass and groaned. "A finch is a bird. A bird has two legs and two wings. It also has a beak. The legs are so he can run, the wings are so he can fly, and the beak so he can eat. He also sings and lays eggs. The eggs are white and round. . . ."

"Can it really fly?" asked Mo.

Willy clapped his hands and the finch flew away. "You see how he can fly?" he called out.

"He flies nicely," said Mo, but she looked at Walter sadly.

Walter noticed it, and he became embarrassed. He sat up and said softly, "Well, soon you'll be flying away, Mo."

"Yes," said Mo.

"That's a shame," said Walter, blushing.

Mo laughed again. "I'll tell my friends all about you," she promised.

"I hope that it won't be so far from the forest line to the

big clearing where her father will come for her," said Otto.

"That'll depend on where Asra will appear in the sky and in what direction we'll have to proceed," said Walter.

"I can't even walk now," groaned Konrad.

"If only Lottie can make it," said Gretel.

Lottie was curled up in the grass with her eyes closed.

"Upon my word," Gretel exclaimed. "She's already fast asleep!"

Lottie sat up with a jerk and forced her eyes open.

"I'm not asleep!" she called out.

"But you're tired, aren't you?" asked Gretel.

"I'm not tired at all; I was just thinking of something," said Lottie.

"Of what?" asked Gretel.

"Of something to eat," said Lottie meekly.

"Are you that hungry?" Gretel asked with concern. Lottie nodded.

"Konrad," called Walter. "Do you still have any caramels?"

"Me?" said Konrad, sitting up. "I . . . I've only two left."

"Give them to Lottie," ordered Walter.

Konrad gave them to Lottie without any fuss. Then he took an apple out of his pocket and ravenously bit into it.

"Where does this apple suddenly come from?" Walter asked suspiciously.

"Oh, that," smacked Konrad. "That's my iron ration."

"That's that half-eaten apple from the market, isn't it?" asked Walter with a knowing grin.

"It would only have turned rotten," Konrad said uneasily. "I just picked it up."

Walter snatched the apple out of his hand. "Let's have it!" he said.

"Don't throw it away," Konrad cried out in dismay. "That would be a crime!"

"Shut up!" said Walter. He broke the apple into eight parts and gave each a piece. "We're all hungry," he said.

The children were glad to have something to eat, and even if it was not much, it tasted very good.

Mo quickly ate her piece of the apple, but then she grew worried and said, "I hope my father will not scold me!"

"Why should he scold you?" Gretel asked with curiosity.

"My father told me that I am not allowed to eat on Earth," Mo confessed feebly. "It could make me sick."

"Apples are good for you," said Walter, trying to comfort her. "They have vitamins."

"What are vitamins?" asked Mo, looking timidly at Walter.

"Vitamins are some stuff without which humans can't live," Walter explained to her, this time eagerly.

"But I am not a human," breathed Mo, and eyed the children cautiously.

"But then what does your father eat when he comes to earth?" asked Otto.

"He always carries pills with him," said Mo.

"Ugh, pills all taste nasty!" Erna said, and turned up her nose in disgust.

"Our pills taste good," said Mo.

"You can have your Asra, if pills are all you have to eat there," said Konrad.

"Why do you always eat nothing but pills?" asked Willy.

Mo was completely stumped. "Why, there is not anything else," she said.

The children would have loved to go on talking about Asra and the pills, but at that point they were attacked by a swarm of mosquitoes, which put an end to their rest.

"Those horrible mosquitoes," complained Erna, slapping herself wildly.

"What a tiny little animal," Mo remarked in fascination. A mosquito had alighted on her leg. Gretel quickly slapped it, and Mo was horrified. "Why did you hit that animal?" she cried out.

"It stings," said Gretel.

"That is no reason to harm it," Mo said reproachfully. Large or small, an animal was an animal to her.

"Such a small animal is no animal," said Otto.

"Let's get away from here," ordered Walter. "The mosquitoes are worse near the swamp."

They went along the edge of the forest for a short distance until they came to a trail.

"This must be the continuation of the field path," Walter guessed.

"Will that take us to the Easter path?" Otto asked skeptically.

"Yes," said Walter, and scanned the sky. "The field path heads due west; we're bound to hit the Easter path."

"How do you know which direction is west?" asked Erna.

"Way over there the sky is red. Where the sun sets is west," said Walter.

Walter went ahead and the others followed, again in single file, as the path was very narrow. It wound through thick underbrush of young spruce and shrubs.

"Ouch! Be careful!" yelled Gretel. "Dope!"

Otto had bent back a twig, and when he let go, it snapped in her face.

"Why don't you watch it!" said Otto.

"Don't follow one another so closely!" called Walter. "Otto, Willy, Konrad, you three break the twigs right and left so that they hang down!"

"Why?" asked Willy.

"That way we'll know that we've been through here before, in case we have to retrace our steps to find another trail."

"A lot of work, this breaking off the twigs," complained Konrad.

"Eeks, a cobweb just got into my hair!" shrieked Erna.

"Holy cats!" cried Otto. "My glasses fell off!" He wanted to break a very thick branch. When he let go, it whipped back and knocked off his glasses.

"My glasses!" howled Otto in despair.

"Look for them; we'll wait!" called Walter.

"How can I look for them if I'm not wearing them?" Otto called back.

Willy, Erna, and Gretel crawled all around searching for Otto's glasses.

"I found them," called Willy.

"Where are they?" asked Otto.

"I've stepped on them!" Willy called triumphantly.

"Then I'm lost!" Otto cried in dismay.

But the glasses were undamaged—by luck they had dropped on a rotten mushroom, which lay squashed on the ground.

Otto cleaned them with tenderness as Walter grew impatient.

"Why can't you clean them while we walk?" he growled.

"If I can't see, I can't walk," insisted Otto. Nevertheless he put them on and continued on his way. But after a few steps he again shouted, "Stop!"

"What the devil is the matter now?" called Walter.

"They stink!" cried Otto.

"Who stinks?" yelled Walter.

"My glasses!" yelled Otto.

"Let them stink," Walter shouted furiously, "as long as you can see something!" He quickly moved on and paid no attention to Otto. The others followed, and Otto had to put up with the smell of his glasses in order not to fall behind.

The trail came to an end abruptly, and a steep wall of rock hindered their progress. It extended from north to south.

"What'll we do now?" asked Otto. He finally took off his glasses, spat on them with fervor, and polished them feverishly.

"Looks pretty steep," Walter said, taken aback.

"You're not going to get *me* up there," murmured Konrad.

"Boy, that's a cinch!" announced Willy, and with that he crawled up the wall like a mountain goat. But he bumped his head against a short, stubby branch, and his hat got pushed over his eyes. With nothing but a handgrip, he dangled on the wall, wiggling with his feet trying to get a toehold.

"Where am I?" he shouted. "I can't see a thing any more!"

Walter climbed up to him, pushed his hat into place, and then both descended.

"Quit playing the hero," Walter snarled at him.

"I've climbed the Thunderpeak all by myself," said Willy.

"That's not true!" cried Erna. "You did not."

Willy just stared at his battered hat. To make matters worse, it now had a deep tear. "A fine mess," he murmured.

"We should go back and look for another trail," said Otto.

"There wasn't any," Walter answered.

"I broke three branches," complained Konrad.

Walter walked along the wall of rock to study it more closely. He disappeared behind a corner, and suddenly the children heard him call, "There are steps here! They're quite easy!"

A sort of staircase, hewn into the rock, led them in a zigzag to the top. It even had a primitive handrail. The children climbed rapidly, but when they reached the top, they discovered that they were standing on a plateau that dropped off steeply on all sides. There was no sign of a trail or steps. Below them lay a thickly wooded gorge hemmed in by precipitous rock walls, and in between they saw only an impenetrable ocean of treetops.

"The Easter path can't be down there," said Walter in a discouraged voice.

"Now we're licked," said Otto with a heavy sigh.

Speechless, they stared into the black abyss.

Eighteen

Not Wide Enough for a Pencil

"We ought to go home," Konrad said with a surly grunt.

"Go ahead then!" Walter challenged him angrily.

"I couldn't get through the swamp alone," Konrad murmured meekly.

"Those rock walls over there don't look so bad," Willy said. "Perhaps the Easter path is just beyond them."

"We'll never make it with Mo and Lottie," said Walter.

"Shall I climb down to the gorge?" asked Willy.

"No, it won't do any good," replied Walter.

"Then we'll have to backtrack to the county road after all," Otto put in with reluctance.

"We can't get through the swamp in the dark," said Walter. He sat down, propped his head on his fists, and watched a spider crawl over his shoe.

"We have to do something! We can't sit here forever!" Erna cried out in despair.

Up here the wind was much stronger than in the forest, and it was considerably cooler. Bats winged silently around their heads. Two tree trunks were rubbing against each other with an ugly creak, and from somewhere came the eerie shriek of a night owl.

"Ugh, how hideous!" squeaked Lottie, covering up her ears.

Mo turned pale. Her eyes grew bigger and bigger. "Are we not going to continue?" she asked nervously.

"No," said Konrad, "you have to stay on earth."

"But I can't live on Earth," Mo said, horrified.

Walter gave Konrad an angry look. "Dope," he snarled.

Konrad was peeved. He had not intended to be mean. Actually he was a goodhearted lad, but, feeling hungry and tired, he was irritable. Again no one spoke.

"I can hear water," said Mo.

"Where?" called Konrad. "I'm dying of thirst."

"Down there," said Mo, and pointed toward the gorge.

The others heard nothing. But Walter walked to the edge of the rocky platform and listened intently. "I think Mo is right; I can hear it too. Hurrah! It's the Hollebrook," he cried out with elation. "Mo must have fantastic ears!"

"What good is the Hollebrook to us?" asked Otto. "I don't feel like taking a dip now."

"The Easter path crosses the Hollebrook, don't you see," Walter explained in an elated tone. "That's where the wooden footbridge is!"

Otto jumped up, excited. "I get it!" he said. "All we need to do is follow the Hollebrook to reach the Easter path."

"You've hit the nail smack on the head, old man," Walter said in high spirits. His courage was revived.

"Yippee!" shouted Willy, and, without any further ado, he slid down the steep slope. He went faster and faster until, with a resounding splash, he landed in the middle of the Hollebrook. "Zowie! It's cold!" came a shout.

The rest of the children descended with great caution, as they had to help Lottie and Mo. They reached the bottom safely and found Willy lying on a rock completely drenched.

"Very refreshing," he said with a sheepish grin. But his teeth were chattering.

With a grunt Konrad flopped on his belly and greedily drank of the clear mountain water. The others also quenched their thirst. Mo cupped her hand and tasted the water.

"Do you drink water on Asra too?" Gretel asked.

"Oh, yes," said Mo, "except that our water has a sweeter flavor."

"I suppose your streams just overflow with soda pop," said Otto mockingly.

The cool drink cheered and revived the children, and they looked at Walter full of expectation. Walter stood near the brook looking rather undecided. He first glanced to the right and then to the left, scratching his head all the while.

"What are you looking for?" Otto asked tensely.

"I don't know whether we should go upstream or downstream. The bridge could be up there or down there. If we head the wrong way now, it's curtains," he said. "We will make only very slow progress. The whole place is full of boulders."

Unperturbed, the waters of the Hollebrook gurgled down the rocky bed. Trunks of fallen trees lay between little waterfalls, which had formed here and there. On both sides towered the steep rock walls of the gorge.

"It's pretty dark down here," Gretel said gloomily.

"And frightfully cold too," said Erna. Her skirt was still damp from the swamp.

"I'm for going downstream," said Otto. "That way, if we miss the bridge, we'll at least be on our way home."

"No," said Walter with grim determination.

"Are we going upstream then?" asked Gretel.

"No," said Walter, even more grimly.

"Then have it your way!" said Konrad, and sat down on a plank lying on top of two small rocks. There was a sharp crack, and he fell over backwards. "Ouch!" he yelled, and angrily hurled the board into the air.

Walter examined the piece with interest. Suddenly, he picked it up and began to dance a jig.

"Yippee!" he roared, obviously beside himself.

The others thought he suddenly had gone stark-raving mad.

"Jeepers creepers!" cried Gretel, terrified.

"Upstream! We have to go upstream!" Walter shouted, waving the board triumphantly over his head.

"How? Why?" the children cried out, dumbfounded.

"This board!" Walter said excitedly. "It's from the foot-bridge. There are nails in it. There are more of them back there; do you see them?"

"Yes," said the children, but they could not understand why this made him so happy.

"Those boards were washed up here with the spring floods," Walter explained. "Therefore, the bridge must be up there." He pointed upstream.

"Why?" asked Konrad. He was a bit slow on the uptake.

"Have you ever seen boards float upstream?" Walter asked laughingly.

"I've never been here before," replied Konrad, completely befuddled.

His stupid answer caused much merriment among the others, and they started happily on their way. But they made slow progress, as they constantly had to climb over big rocks and fallen tree trunks. The rock wall along which they were moving angled steadily toward the Hollebrook until finally they came to a dead end.

"No room any more," said Walter. "We'll have to cross over."

On the other side the rock wall stood farther back from the stream. This time, before wading across, the children remembered to take off their shoes and socks, which made their footing more secure on the slippery stones under water. In order to have their hands free in case they should slip, they made Otto's jacket into a kind of sack. They put all the shoes and socks into it and hung the whole thing around Otto's neck. This made him furious, but as it was his own jacket all his complaining proved futile.

When they waded through the brook, the children skillfully stepped from rock to rock so that only their feet got wet. They reached the other shore without mishap and walked over rock slabs worn smooth by the water. As they came around a corner they stopped dumbfounded. Here the world suddenly seemed to have come to an end. The rock walls on both sides of the stream projected so far that they almost touched. All one could see was a black gap no

wider than the width of the hand. Only at the bottom was
the opening wider, but there the Hollebrook came shoot-
ing out with a deafening roar.

"That's the gorge!" Walter shouted.

"I'll get through!" Willy shouted without fear.

At this spot, the brook was making such a noise that the
children could only make themselves understood with the
greatest difficulty.

"You couldn't even jam a pencil through there," shouted
Otto.

Walter put one leg into the hole where the brook came
roaring out and called: "It's only up to my knee!" Then, to

explore farther, he put his head through the gap and looked into the gorge.

"I think we can make it. If you hug the wall, you can squeeze through. Just two steps and you're through the gorge!"

"Wait, let me try," called Willy. He jumped into the hole, pressed close against the wall, and pushed himself sideways into the gap. The water churned angrily around his legs, but Willy was unperturbed. He disappeared from sight, and a moment later they could hear him call, "Whoopee! The bridge is behind here! Follow me!"

Walter rubbed his hands with satisfaction. "Never throw in the towel too soon!" he remarked.

"Willy," he yelled. "Listen, I'll hand you Lottie; the water is too deep for her!" He picked up Lottie and passed her to Willy. Lottie closed her eyes, plugged her ears with her fingers, and shrieked. But she bravely submitted to everything. Willy took hold of her and skillfully carried her to a rock beside the brook, where he put her down.

Mo also was too small; the water would have reached to her hips and might have knocked her under. Walter lifted her up, but, although he mustered all his strength, he was unable to get her close to Willy. She was too heavy.

"Put her on your shoulders!" shouted Gretel.

Walter tried this, but the gap was so narrow that her knees would not pass through.

"Make her stand on your shoulders," Otto yelled.

But that proved no more successful, as the gap was even narrower at the top.

"I have an idea," called Willy. "Walter, hold out your arms!" Walter extended his arms, and Willy reached for them and grasped his hands. "This is a bridge!" he shouted. "Mo can walk on it!"

"That's the boy, Willy," Walter exclaimed admiringly. He bent forward, and with Erna's and Gretel's assistance Mo climbed on his back. She stepped on the "bridge" that Willy and Walter had constructed with their arms, and, clinging to the wall, she gingerly pushed herself through the gap. She was not the least bit afraid and called: "This is a lot of fun!"

Nevertheless, she had to sit on Willy's head until he could free himself from Walter. Then Willy lifted her off and sat her down next to Lottie.

"You did that very well," Mo said with a grateful smile.

Willy bowed like a clown in a circus. His hat fell into the water and with dizzying speed disappeared in the hole beneath the rock.

"My hat!" shrieked Willy.

Walter retrieved it in the nick of time at the other side. He put it on, but when he felt water trickling down his neck, he quickly handed it back to Willy.

"Now it's Gretel's turn! Then Erna's!" he ordered. "I'll watch on this side so they won't get dragged under!"

Gretel tied up her skirt and pushed through the gorge. The thundering roar and the damp, cold rock walls did not amuse her, but she squeezed through without difficulty.

Erna did not have to bother about her skirt, still damp from the pot hole into which she had fallen. She too managed without trouble, which filled her with pride.

Walter followed with ease. Now it was Konrad's turn. But he did not get very far. "Help! I'm stuck!" he roared.

He was hopelessly wedged in and unable to move in any direction.

Nineteen

Too Many Stars in the Sky

"Help!" roared Konrad, holding his hand out to Walter. Walter grabbed it and pulled while Otto, standing behind Konrad, put his shoulder against him. But Konrad only got wedged in tighter, and he cried: "I'm suffocating! Let go of me!"

"Give it all you've got!" shouted Walter, and almost tore his arm out.

"I can't! I'm too fat!" groaned Konrad.

Now Walter pressed his shoulders against him while Otto did the pulling until Konrad once more stood helpless at the entrance of the gorge with water roaring up to his knees.

"Perhaps you can crawl through the hole?" yelled Otto.

"Into that boiling rapid?" Konrad called out, worried.

"Why don't you try?" Otto encouraged him.

Konrad was fat, but he was no coward, so, with desperate determination, he dove headfirst into the hole where the Hollebrook came roaring out. Immediately the current pushed him downstream, and like a small barrel, he drifted against a boulder. The water splashed over his head, and he shouted: "I'm drowning! I can't get up!"

Otto quickly waded up to him and pulled him free. "Try again!" he called.

"No," gurgled Konrad, and spouted a quart of water.

Meanwhile, on the other side of the gorge, Walter and Willy had an idea how to help Konrad.

"The only way," Walter suggested, "would be to pull him through with something."

"How about my fishline?" shouted Willy with eagerness. He pulled the line out of his pocket.

"Is it strong enough?" Walter asked skeptically.

"Boy," exclaimed Willy, "and how! I can catch the biggest pike on it."

"Let's have it!" said Walter. To make sure, he doubled it. Then he hurried back to the gorge and called: "Hey, Konrad, we'll pull you through the hole with Willy's fishline!"

"I'm no fish," answered Konrad indignantly.

"If you don't want to, you'll have to go home alone," shouted Walter.

"No!" Konrad shouted back in horror. "Throw it to me."

Walter let the water carry the free end of the string to Konrad. Konrad picked it up and held onto it with both hands. Then he crouched and waited for the pull.

Willy, Walter, Gretel, and Erna all took hold of the fishline and began to pull. The line parted, and all four fell backwards into the water. They jumped out and shook themselves. Erna and Gretel shrieked: "Ugh, ugh!" Lottie clapped her hands and squealed with delight. Even Mo could not help laughing.

"Stop your laughing!" snorted Erna in a rage. "What's

so funny about it?" Her beautiful red hair clung to her face like a wet mop.

Lottie and Mo were frightened and stopped laughing. Gretel tried to squeeze the water out of her dress like a sponge. Willy met Walter's angry look with a sheepish smile.

"Your fishline isn't worth a hoot," Walter snarled.

"Konrad isn't a pike either," protested Willy.

"If only we had a strong rope . . ." sighed Walter, rubbing his soaked hair. His eyes fell on Mo's coat. He stumbled over to her and asked: "Mo, do you still need your coat?"

"Oh, yes," replied Mo. "Don't you remember? It belongs to the doll in the museum. I am obliged to bring it home."

"Too bad," said Walter, "because it might have served to help Konrad. We could make a strong rope out of it and save him."

At once Mo took off the coat and handed it to Walter. "Please, please," she begged, "save Konrad! Konrad is a good human. I will tell my father that we had to help him. After all, the doll is just a doll. It is not alive, is it?"

"No," said Walter. He was very touched. With great effort he tore the coat and the remaining sleeve into strips and knotted them securely together.

"Willy, give it a good pull to see if it will hold," he ordered.

Willy heaved with all his might, and Walter was pleased. The rope held. He walked up to the gorge and shouted: "Konrad, we have a firm rope, guaranteed to hold!"

"Let me have it! I'll hang myself with it!" Konrad called back. He had lost all confidence.

"You're a drip," Gretel called in a fury.

"Who?" Konrad yelled.

"You!" answered Gretel.

"Wait, I'm coming!" roared Konrad in anger, and seized the rope of cloth that Walter had thrown to him. Again, Willy, Walter, Gretel, and Erna heaved, backing up step by step until at last Konrad's head appeared. He snorted like a seal. Walter let go of the coat and quickly grabbed Konrad by his hair, while the others took him by his hands and arms. Then they happily got him through the hole. Exhausted, Konrad slumped on a rock. He tilted his head from one side to the other to let the water run out of his ears. His rage had cooled off.

"I'll show her who's a drip," he muttered faintly.

Gretel laughed tauntingly. "Why don't you try," she hissed. "I'll scratch and bite!"

Now it was still up to Otto to squeeze through the gorge. He was short and had a hard time of it. The water came almost to his thighs. But he was tough and skillful and worked his way through slowly, but surely. In fact, all would have gone smoothly if the jacket containing the shoes and stockings, which he carried on his back, had not got caught on a sharp ledge. He jerked it in desperation, and the sack burst open, spilling the shoes and stockings into the roaring brook.

"Holy catfish!" howled Otto. "There go all our shoes and stockings."

"My sandals! Save my sandals!" cried Gretel.

Otto vanished, but after a while he returned and announced: "They're gone! I can't see them anywhere!"

The children were terrified. This was an awful catastrophe. Although they were used to going barefoot out-of-doors, they realized only too well that shoes and stockings cost a lot of money.

"Mommy will scold us terribly!" wailed Gretel. "How can she buy us new ones!"

Erna was the most upset. "Mother bought my shoes at Wurmbach's in Pocksburg," she cried.

"Anyway, they were much too stylish for you," remarked Willy, but he was no longer quite his cheerful self.

"They were *not* too stylish," sulked Erna tearfully.

"We'll have to proceed barefoot," Walter said, shaken.

"On all those pebbles?" said Konrad gruffly. "After all, I'm no fakir!"

"Did my shoes and stockings drown too?" asked Mo anxiously.

"I'm afraid so," confessed Walter.

Mo was very perturbed. "Now the doll has no coat, no shoes, and no stockings any more," she said sadly.

Walter pulled Mo's red cap out of his pants pocket and put it on her head. "But the doll still has the cap," he said shyly.

Otto got a cool reception.

"Why didn't you pay more attention?" Gretel jumped at him, speaking with fury.

"Why didn't *you* carry the jacket?" Otto replied hotly.

"My shoes had rubber soles," Lottie said, worried.

All the reproaches were of no use. Meanwhile, it had grown quite dark, and many stars had already appeared in the sky. The children cast a last glance in the direction of the fatal gorge and then moved on. From here, the bridge was no longer distant, but the approach to it was tiresome and painful because of the many big and small rocks.

Mo, with her small, tender feet, could hardly walk at all on the loose stones. Gretel and Erna had to help her by holding her arms. It was only after they had climbed the slope to the Easter path that they all drew a deep breath of relief.

"It isn't as bad here," observed Walter.

"Like this it's very nice," agreed Mo, finding grass on the path instead of rocks.

"But be careful not to step on a thorny twig!" Walter warned her. "It is dark. Better follow close behind me."

Confidently, though with a wary eye to the ground, Mo trotted behind him. At last, they saw the big clearing where they had discovered Mo in the morning glimmering through the trees and excitedly ran toward it.

The first thing Otto did was to climb under the tree to look for the mushrooms that he had left behind in the morning.

"The mushrooms are still here," he reported with joy.

"Bring them here!" Konrad called eagerly. "We'll eat them."

However, Walter would have none of it. "They're too old," he explained. "Besides, we have no time. We still have

to find the big meadow where Mo's father will arrive." He took Mo by the hand and led her to the middle of the clearing from where they could have a good view of the stars.

"Where is Asra?" he asked tensely.

The children rushed up and stared at Mo, full of expectancy.

Mo contemplated the sky at length. She turned in a circle and looked and looked. Her face grew longer, her eyes bigger, and finally she stammered: "I don't know where Asra is."

"What?" cried the children, dumbfounded.

"How . . . why not?" Walter blurted, completely unnerved. "You surely must know!"

"There are too many stars in the sky," Mo said faintly. She sat down in the grass and glanced uneasily at the others.

Twenty

West Is Opposite to East

The children did not know what to say.

From the forest came the cracking of twigs, as when an animal breaks through the underbrush. Two glowing eyes blinked for a moment from the thicket, and from somewhere sounded the cooing of a ring dove.

"That's a fine mess!" Otto murmured in a daze, and gave Mo a reprimanding look over the top of his glasses.

"What do you mean when you say there are too many stars in the sky, Mo?" Walter asked hoarsely.

"I do not know which star is Asra," Mo answered meekly, and again gazed at the sky, feeling at a loss.

"But your father couldn't have called to you to keep walking toward Asra when you don't have any idea where Asra is," Walter pointed out.

"I did know," Mo said faintly. "He always pointed out Asra to me as we flew through space. But from there everything looked quite different."

"How come?" asked the children.

Mo frowned and thought for a long time. Then she said: "The sky looked pitch-black. The stars were all around. The sun, too, was there all the time."

"But where was Asra?" Otto interrupted impatiently.

"Asra was big and fat," said Mo. "But from here everything looks quite different." Mo lapsed into an uneasy silence.

The children, equally at a loss, stared at the sky.

"Perhaps *that* is Asra!" suggested Konrad, pointing to a bright star directly overhead.

"Don't talk baloney," jeered Otto. "We can't walk toward something that's right above us!"

"That's right," Walter admitted, racking his brain. "It has to be a star that is lower in the sky."

"Perhaps that is Asra!" said Gretel, pointing at a big star appearing just above the horizon.

"How should we know?" snarled Otto. "It hasn't got the name printed on it."

"Asra can't be so hard to find," remarked Willy, and made a few quick turns to take in all the stars. But then he grinned and had no more to say.

"We'll never find Asra!" whimpered Erna.

"I'll head for home," grunted Konrad. Instead he sat down and just stared at the spruce where the mushrooms lay.

"Me too," said Erna in a huff. "I've got to dry my hair or I'll look a fright tomorrow." Her hair was still dripping, like a wet mop. The children were all soaked. Only Mo and Lottie had stayed dry. Luckily, in the forest it was much warmer than in the gorge of the Hollebrook. At least they weren't cold any more.

"I'm going now!" said Erna with a challenging look at Willy.

"So long!" said Willy, and lifted his hat in mock salute.

"You must come too!" Erna shouted angrily.

"Me?" said Willy. "Can't you manage to dry your hair by yourself?"

Walter was silent and lost in thought.

"We'll all go home," said Otto with a defiant air. "Mo must come along. What are we fiddling around here for?"

"Mo can't live on earth. She's bound to get sick and die," said Walter.

"Oh, no!" cried Lottie, and began to sob. She was ready to drop with exhaustion.

"Perhaps she'll get used to earth," Konrad said without conviction. "After all, she did eat some of the apple."

Otto had begun to waver. Walter's words had made a deep impression on him. He, too, did not want Mo to die. "It's strange that she doesn't know where to look for Asra," he said reluctantly.

"How can Mo help it that the stars look different from earth!" cried Gretel in a fury, and excitedly flung her hair behind her neck. "Her father should have told her where Asra is."

"My father was very excited because I fell from our space ship," Mo said timidly.

"I'm sure Walter will know what we should do," said Gretel to comfort Mo.

"You don't believe that yourself," exclaimed Otto.

"I do too!" Gretel snapped defiantly.

"I don't believe anything, except that my pants are wet," moaned Otto. He took off his coat and tried to dry his pants with it.

"Why don't you all go home?" Walter said with determination. "I'll stay here with Mo."

"I'll stay too," Gretel chimed in.

"Me too," piped Lottie.

The others demurred. They would have preferred to go home, but Walter was their best friend and they did not want to leave him in the lurch.

"Walter must believe in miracles," Otto said cautiously.

"Perhaps all the stars aren't out yet," said Walter.

"It's dark, and those are all the stars there are," said Otto.

"I've got an idea!" Willy called. "Let's make a huge fire! Maybe Mo's father will see it and come here!"

"A fire would be swell. We could have a chestnut roast," Konrad said gleefully.

"We're not allowed to light a fire in the forest. It's against the law," explained Walter.

"We have no matches anyhow," said Otto.

"I've got another idea," Willy called out.

"What?" asked the children, though they were not very hopeful.

"Mo must have come from somewhere," said Willy.

"Sure," agreed Gretel, "she came from Asra."

"But she must have come from some direction," Willy went on, unruffled. "From the west, or east, or south, or north."

"There are no directions in the universe, you dope," said Otto with a grunt. The children were disappointed.

But Willy refused to be discouraged. "From what direction did you come, Mo? From the west, east, south, or north?"

"I don't know what that is," Mo said sadly. "My father told me to walk toward Asra immediately after sunset."

"Hey!" Walter called suddenly. The others watched him tensely. "I've got it! Immediately after sunset!"

"Immediately after sunset there are no stars out," Otto said disdainfully.

"There *are*!" cried Walter, overjoyed. He pounded his fist against his hand. "The Evening Star! The Evening Star!"

"What about the Evening Star," the children asked, all excited.

"Immediately after the sun has set, one can see the Evening Star, long before any other stars appear!" Walter cried jubilantly.

"Boy!" cried Willy. "I can tell the Evening Star too; I see it every morning."

"Mo, Mo?" called Walter. "Do you come from the Evening Star?"

"I come from Asra," said Mo, confused. By now she, too, was excited.

"I'm sure Asra is the Evening Star," Walter said. "There is no other star right after sunset. Your father knew that you couldn't possibly mistake it!"

"My father is very clever," said Mo, and jumped with delight.

"But where is the Evening Star?" asked Gretel, worried.

"In the west!" Walter beamed. "The Evening Star is always where the sun sets."

"Jeepers," shouted Willy, "the Evening Star is in the west!"

Walter scanned the sky in all directions. "Oh, nuts!" he exclaimed unexpectedly.

"What's the matter?" the others asked.

"Now I can't remember which way west lies," Walter said, baffled.

"But you knew a short while ago!" said Gretel.

"Then one could still see where the sun had set," Walter said, discouraged. "Now one can't see a thing. Without the glow, it looks the same all over."

"Perhaps the wind is from the west," suggested Willy. He sucked his finger and held it up in the air.

"If the wind is from the west, how can we tell when we don't know where west is?" remarked Otto with finality.

"The wind is always from the west; my father says so," insisted Willy stubbornly. He again licked his finger and held it up even higher. However, this was no help either, for the simple reason that meanwhile it had become dead calm.

"Let's climb on top of those rocks!" called Walter. "Perhaps we can find the Evening Star from there. Sometimes it stands very low."

Willy was on top in a jiffy, and Walter and Otto climbed up after him. Konrad alone remained sitting in the grass in a mood of defiance.

"Why don't you help too?" Gretel called scornfully. "Perhaps *you* will find the Evening Star!"

"Why should *I* know!" said Konrad, disgruntled. "In the evening all stars are evening stars."

"Lazybones!" said Gretel angrily.

Erna watched the boys intently, and Gretel ran up to the rock and called: "Do you see it?"

"No," answered Walter. "It must have disappeared already."

"I see the moon!" shouted Willy with a friendly smile. The moon was rising full and big above the rock wall of the Hollebrook.

"The moon!" Walter roared in ecstasy. "Mo is safe!"

"Is the moon the Evening Star?" asked Erna, amazed.

"No," answered Walter, "but now I know in which direction to walk!"

"How so?" Konrad asked, getting to his feet. Now he became interested.

"A full moon always rises in the east!" explained Walter. "We learned that in school."

"I didn't," insisted Konrad.

"But we're supposed to go west, not east!" Gretel maintained.

Walter took a daring leap from the boulder. "West is opposite to east!" he cried breathlessly. "If we walk and keep the moon behind us, it's like walking toward Asra."

"Yippee!" Willy shouted with joy. In his enthusiasm he shoved Otto over the edge. He landed on Gretel's back, and both fell over. Gretel jumped up and pounded him with both fists.

"Why don't you watch where you're going, you dope!" she shouted.

Otto was visibly unnerved. "Did you hurt yourself?" he asked anxiously.

"No," scolded Gretel, "but I got into something." She was covered from head to foot with burs.

In a trice, the children picked off all the burs, and then they wanted to be on their way. In the meantime, Lottie had fallen fast asleep. She was lying under a spruce and was slumbering peacefully as if she were at home in her little bed.

Gretel shook her gently. "Lottie," she called.

But Lottie could not be wakened so easily.

"Could not she sleep a bit longer?" Mo begged, feeling sorry for her.

"We couldn't wait till then," said Gretel. "Once she falls asleep, she'll sleep till doomsday."

"Lottie! You've got to wake up!" called Walter.

Startled, Lottie sat bolt upright. "Yes?" she whispered drowsily.

"You promised not to get tired," said Gretel.

"But I'm not tired," said Lottie. 'I just took a quick snooze."

She rubbed her eyes and yawned. "I was dreaming of the potato soup."

"We've got to push on," said Gretel. "We know now where Mo's father is arriving."

"Oh, great!" Lottie exclaimed, and jumped to her feet. "Where does he arrive?" she asked eagerly.

"In the west," said Gretel.

Walter looked around for the moon and then, whistling a gay tune, marched into the forest.

The moon shone almost as bright as a searchlight, and

the children made rapid headway. The trees were spaced wide apart, and there was no underbrush. The forest animals apparently had all gone to sleep. Everything was still. Even the rustling of the leaves had stopped. Only once in a while did Walter stop to look at the moon to make sure that they were keeping it in back of them. Suddenly he froze in his steps and called under his breath: "Stop, don't move. There are animals back there!"

In the background they could vaguely see some game running through the woods, but it quickly disappeared, and the children continued, much relieved.

"Those were deer," Willy said cheerfully.

"Nonsense," said Otto. "Those were wild boar. I could hear them snort."

"That snort was Konrad," said Gretel.

"I'm no bulldog," said Konrad, offended.

Actually, neither Konrad nor the boars had snorted, but Mo, who was panting heavily. She sat down and dropped her head.

"I cannot walk any more," she sighed.

The children gathered around her, terrified.

"What's troubling you?" asked Walter anxiously.

"The Earth air is getting thicker and thicker," said Mo, gasping.

Gretel kneeled beside her and put her hand on Mo's forehead, as she had seen her mother do. "Mo feels very hot," she said. "Stick out your tongue, Mo."

"Why?" asked Mo, astonished.

"One always has to show one's tongue when one is sick," Otto said firmly.

"My tongue is in good order," said Mo, and pressed her lips together. Apparently she was ashamed to show her tongue.

"I, too, have to show my tongue all the time!" observed Lottie.

"My legs are in bad order," said Mo.

"I'll carry you," said Walter.

"Oh, no," said Mo. "I am too heavy."

"You're not a bit heavy," said Walter, and carried her pickaback.

"You are very wet," said Mo.

"I fell in the water, don't you remember?" said Walter, and plodded on, but not as briskly as before.

"I did not want to laugh," said Mo, "but it was very funny."

"That's all right," croaked Walter, who was panting heavily. "It is always a joke when someone falls in the water."

"I am very sad that you have to carry me," said Mo.

Walter didn't respond but clenched his teeth. With each step, Mo seemed to get bigger and heavier. By now he was panting harder than Mo, and he felt his knees giving out. Unable to go on, he was just thinking of letting her down when Willy let out a shout. "Yippee! The open field! We're here!"

With every ounce of remaining strength, Walter stumbled out of the woods and gently put Mo on the ground. Then he, too, sat down and struggled to catch his breath.

Before them lay a vast plateau extending to the distant timberlands on the horizon. A few scraggly oak trees,

twisted by the wind, stood in the foreground. The only other growth was meadow grass covering the ground between widely scattered, massive boulders.

By now the moon was high, and the barren, desolate landscape was drenched in an eerie light. The oak trees cast a weird shadow, and where the forest began, it was completely dark.

The children looked all around, but they saw no trace of a space ship.

Twenty-One

Now, Home at Once

Mo sat in the grass without moving. She was breathing heavily.

The children made long faces, and even Gretel became suspicious. She eyed her brother nervously, but Walter avoided her stare and pretended to be completely absorbed in studying his big toe.

"This is where the foxes kiss each other good night," observed Otto after a while. Then they all fell silent again. Willy, too, had lost his zest.

Walter gave Mo a long, searching stare and said: "Your father didn't come."

"Perhaps he still will come," Mo said meekly.

"How long does it take him from the moon to here?" Walter asked.

"He is usually very punctual," said Mo.

"There is somebody coming!" called Willy under his breath. Scarcely a thing escaped his lynx-eyes.

"Where?" the others asked with a jolt.

"There!" Willy pointed to the edge of the forest.

At that moment, some two hundred feet away, a strange creature emerged from under the trees and then stood still.

It looked human—in fact it had two legs and two arms and it even wore a jacket with a turned-up collar. But in a spooky way the head was missing. The children sat petrified.

"Is that your father?" whispered Walter.

"No," replied Mo. "My father has a head."

Lottie clutched Gretel and whimpered, "I'm scared!"

Gretel was terrified herself and said nothing. Erna had turned white as a sheet.

"Perhaps it's a scarecrow," stuttered Konrad.

"Since when can a scarecrow walk?" Otto croaked hoarsely.

"It's a human being," said Walter in a dubious tone. He wanted to reassure the others but did not feel too relaxed himself.

"That's no human!" shrieked Erna in wild terror. "It's a spook! Help!" She wanted to run away but tripped and fell.

A head with white hair appeared out of the jacket, and the creature ran toward them, waving and calling.

"Miss Tim!" exclaimed Walter, stupefied. He jumped to his feet.

"Children! Children! There you are, at last, you runaways!" Miss Tim called, delighted. She wore ski pants and had a walking stick in her hand and a knapsack on her back as if she were going for a mountain climb in the middle of the night. "Do tell, where on earth have you been all this time?" Miss Tim asked with a sigh of relief. Shaking her head, she confronted the children.

The children were still speechless.

"And why are you soaking wet?" Miss Tim asked, horrified.

"We fell into the water," admitted Walter.

"Everything fell into the water," Otto murmured.

"Your parents are desperately looking for you everywhere," said Miss Tim. "They are worried to death."

"Why?" asked the children in surprise.

"Well, it's very late," said Miss Tim. "You should have been home hours ago."

"Where are they looking for us?" asked Walter uneasily.

"In the forest," said Miss Tim. "I told them that you most likely had gone to the Gackenburg Meadows, but they wouldn't believe me. So I struck out on my own and came here to see whether you had already arrived. Those mosquitoes almost ate me alive. I pulled my jacket over my head, but even so I'm bitten all over."

"How did you know that we were going to the Gackenburg Meadows?" Walter asked, completely amazed.

"Why, Sergeant Klotz was looking for you, so I asked him what the trouble was. Well, that's how I learned about everything, and so I went directly to see your parents, because I was worried about you. What a remarkable story they had to tell me!"

Miss Tim gave Mo, still perched in the grass, a searching glance. The moonlight cast a silvery glow on her blonde hair. Her face was waxen, and she sadly looked at the sky.

"Hm," was all Miss Tim managed to say, and then turned again to Walter. "Your father remembered that immediately after sundown you wanted to walk toward Asra. . . ."

"Do you, too, believe in Asra, Miss Tim?" Walter interrupted hopefully.

However, Miss Tim said amiably: "Well . . . we'll discuss that later, Walter. Now, as I was saying, immediately after sundown there is only Venus in the sky, correct? I knew at once that it could only be the Gackenburg Meadows. . . ."

"But Asra is the Evening Star!" interjected Gretel.

"The Evening Star *is* Venus," Miss Tim enlightened them.

"Oh, really?" chorused the children. They had never heard anything of Venus before.

"Well, how did *you* know about the Evening Star?" Miss Tim asked curiously.

"We didn't find it," said Walter. "All we knew was that it should be in the west, so we kept walking in that direction."

"And you even knew where west is? At night, in the forest?" exclaimed Miss Tim in admiration.

"The full moon rises in the east," said Walter modestly. "We learned that in school."

"Well, there, you see! School is good for something, after all, don't you think?" said Miss Tim.

"Oh, yes," the children willingly admitted. Only Konrad did not share the general enthusiasm about school. Twice he had failed to be promoted.

Miss Tim looked at Mo again. She hesitated for a moment but then walked up and kneeled beside her.

"Hello, Mo!" she said cordially. "I heard that you're from Asra."

"Do you want to lock me up now?" Mo asked nervously.

"No! No! No!" exclaimed Miss Tim, feigning indignation.

"Nobody wants to lock you up! Tell me, where is your necklace? I understand you have a beautiful one."

"Walter has it," said Mo.

"It's here!" called Walter, and tapped his pants pocket.

"Be sure you don't lose it!" said Miss Tim.

"Oh, no," called Walter, much frightened.

"Well, Mo, are you still waiting for your father?" asked Miss Tim, and gently stroked her hair.

"I will have to," Mo said, ill at ease.

"What will we do if your father doesn't come?" asked Miss Tim, apparently much concerned.

"That would be awful," Mo said sadly. "Then he could not send me any pills." She was gasping for air like a fish out of water.

"You know, Mo," said Miss Tim tenderly, "I was thinking that you would come to my house. All right? I discussed it with the policeman. I have two cunning cats, a canary bird, and masses of pretty flowers. I also have a cozy little bed for you. You will feel very comfy in it—and tomorrow the world will look rosier!"

"I have a very nice bed on Asra," said Mo, and eyed Miss Tim suspiciously.

Miss Tim quickly rose and became serious. "Children," she said with determination, "I must now call your parents."

"Please, not yet!" begged Walter. "Only five minutes more, Miss Tim! Mo's father must arrive any moment now."

"Why, Walter, do you really still believe in that fairy tale of Asra?" asked Miss Tim, perplexed.

"Oh, yes!" called Walter, surprised. "Why shouldn't such a thing exist?"

Miss Tim put her hand on his shoulder. "Walter," she said, "Mo is very sick. She doesn't know what she is saying."

"It's only that she can't stand the air on earth," said Walter hastily. "Mo is wonderful. She surely is not lying. She . . . she is much better than we are," he added, feeling embarrassed and turning dark crimson.

For a moment Miss Tim looked at him quizzically and then gave him a friendly smile. "All right then, Walter, another five minutes. But no longer!" she said.

"Oh, thanks a lot!" called Walter happily.

But at the same moment came the sound of many voices. There was the crackling of twigs, and the beams of flashlights came flickering through the trees. The children wheeled around and stared.

"There they are! There they are!" someone shouted excitedly, and the parents and neighbors came running toward the field from the right and the left. Out in front of all of them were Mr. and Mrs. Brenner. Then followed Mr. Hofer, Mr. and Mrs. Langmueller, and old Mr. Borgmann, who still was very chipper. Bringing up the rear were Miss Beck, fat Mrs. Paul and Mrs. Reuter, as well as Mr. Aufhauser, the mail carrier, Mr. and Mrs. Grobschmidt, and many more. Even Miss Wambacher, the piano teacher, had joined the rescue party.

Considerably farther back the police sergeant appeared. He was limping, as he had stubbed his big toe against a tree root, and although it was quite cool, he was perspiring more than ever. "Hold on to them! Hold on to them!" he roared from a distance.

As a matter of fact, he did not have to worry. The children had no intention of escaping from their parents.

"Jimminy crickets!" murmured Otto. "We'd better quickly get some padding under the seat of our pants."

Mr. and Mrs. Brenner fell upon their children and hugged them warmly.

"Well, thank the Lord! We've got you back!" said Mr. Brenner joyfully.

Mrs. Brenner kept hugging Gretel and Lottie. "Children, oh children! How we worried!" she said.

"I'm not a bit tired," chirped Lottie.

Mr. Hofer shook his head at Konrad. "What a rascal you are!" he said, but he, too, was happy to have him back.

"Is there any food left?" Konrad asked anxiously.

Mr. and Mrs. Langmueller scolded Erna and Willy a bit, but really only for the sake of discipline. Erna turned up her nose, and Willy just grinned sheepishly.

Mr. Borgmann stroked his beard with his trembling hand and repeated over and over: "Main thing, they're well. Main thing, they're well!" But when the parents discovered that the children were soaking wet and wore no shoes or stockings, they became a bit angry.

"My goodness," cried Mrs. Brenner, "you'll catch your death of cold!"

"Now, home at once," ordered Mr. Brenner.

"Couldn't we wait a bit longer?" Walter begged stubbornly.

"Let's have no more of that, and that's final," Mr. Brenner shouted angrily.

"Just five minutes more, Father," Walter implored.

"The boy is crazy too," murmured the crowd, shocked.

"The little one has cast a spell on the children!" shrieked Miss Beck.

"You've had nothing to eat all day," Mrs. Brenner said. "There is potato soup at home and then right to bed!"

"One should take them one by one and give them a good spanking!" Miss Beck cried acidly. "That's what they need!"

Miss Tim suddenly turned on Miss Beck angrily: *"You* will keep your mouth shut! The children did nothing evil. They believed in Asra and wanted to help the child. For that they don't deserve any punishment."

"Oh, *you!*" shrieked Miss Beck. "You always put on airs, just because you once were a teacher!"

"I'm proud of it," Miss Tim answered with dignity. "I'm sure I have a better understanding of children than you do!"

At last the sergeant came limping along. "Where is the little girl with the necklace?" he roared right off.

Greatly surprised, the people looked around for Mo. In the general excitement they had completely forgotten about her.

"Where is she?" Mr. Brenner called, perplexed.

Mo had disappeared.

"That's strange," Miss Tim said. "She was sitting here in the grass."

Walter knew where Mo was, but he stubbornly kept quiet. It so happened that the moment Mo spied the policeman, she ran into the field and scrambled up an oak tree. She had climbed near the top and tried to hide herself among the branches. But the branch on which she was perched broke off, and she slid onto the one below, clutching it in desperation. Unfortunately, the sergeant heard her. He limped up to the tree and called: "In the name of the law I command you to come down immediately!"

"You are a bad man," yelled Mo.

"Come down here," roared the policeman, and shook the tree.

Miss Tim ran up. "You will stop this at once, Sergeant; she might fall off!"

The sergeant was determined to climb up the tree, but when he stepped on the first branch, it broke off immediately, and he crashed into a thistle bush. "Ouch," he yelled, frantically pulling the thistles from the seat of his pants.

"That child will be the death of me yet!" he groaned.

"Child, come on down! We only want to help you," called Mr. and Mrs. Brenner affably.

Instead, Mo climbed still higher. "No," she cried, "my father is coming!"

"Dear child, your father is NOT coming," Mr. Brenner called in exasperation.

"He is too!" Mo suddenly burst out jubilantly. "I can hear him! There is that grumble and rumble! That grumble and rumble! They are all coming! I can even see them now! There they are! There they are!"

But the parents and people heard nothing and saw nothing.

"The poor child!" murmured Mrs. Brenner, feeling sorry for her.

"My father is coming! My father is coming! My father is coming!" shouted Mo, overcome with joy.

"Now the child has gone completely bats!" announced Mr. Hofer.

"Why don't you call the fire department!" shrieked Miss Beck.

"That's it! That's it! That's what we should do," shouted the people.

Then, without warning, Willy broke into a loud cheer: "Yippee! Yippee!! They're really coming!!" And, with complete abandon, he threw his hat high into the air.

"They're really coming," said Walter, deeply moved as he looked up to the stars, completely enthralled.

Twenty-Two

A Shower of Meteors

In the beginning it merely looked like a shower of meteors. But, instead of vanishing, they became bigger and brighter. In a few seconds they resembled golden balls glittering in the sun. There were hundreds, even thousands of them. When they penetrated the shadow of the earth, they reflected the moonlight and suddenly turned silvery. Quickly they grew into huge balls, hurtling toward the meadow with incredible speed. Now one could hear the howling and hissing as they shot through the air, and then they were there, descending slowly. Just above the ground they all stood completely still as if touched by a magic wand. Hatches opened, and from each of the space ships emerged tall, broad-shouldered figures clad in metallic, glittering suits.

The parents and their neighbors turned pale. The men took off their hats; the women fell on their knees and folded their hands. Even the sergeant took off his cap.

Miss Beck gasped, "Oh," and fainted away. But nobody paid any attention to her. Only Miss Tim kept her composure, in a manner of speaking, but her hands trembled, and she murmured without stopping, "Oh my God! Oh my God! Oh my God!"

The children stood with their mouths open and their eyes popping and looked at the space ships in a trance.

The figures that had jumped out remained motionless next to the space ships as though they were waiting for something. They looked like human beings, except that they were much taller, taller by at least a head than the police sergeant, who was very tall. From one of the space ships that had landed close by stepped a man who was dressed like a human being. His hair was blond, his eyes were violet-blue, and his features noble. He approached Miss Tim with quick, elastic steps and addressed her politely: "Good day! We are from Asra, called Venus by Earth people!"

Miss Tim walked toward him. "I greet you, in the name of earth and humanity!" she said solemnly, though with a slight quiver in her voice.

"Many thanks," said the tall man from Asra amicably. "I hope we did not frighten you too much. I have brought my friends along because we have to return from here directly to Asra, if we still want to make it. We did not expect to meet people here."

"We happen to be here quite by accident," Miss Tim said. "My name is Josephine Tim, librarian of the Kummersville public library, formerly headmistress of the girls' school in Tifflelake." She held out her hand.

"Pleased to meet you!" responded the man, and shook Miss Tim's hand. He seemed to know the customs on earth. "My name is Tono Kalumba, grand master of Earth science on Asra. I came to fetch my daughter. Through a mishap she fell on Earth."

"Your daughter is sitting in a tree," said Miss Tim.

"What, again?" exclaimed Mo's father and laughed. "She does the same on Asra. But children will be children, right? The same on Earth as on Asra. But in which tree is she, may I ask?"

"Up in that oak!" said Miss Tim.

Mo came scurrying down. In all the haste her beautiful silk dress got caught on a pointed branch and tore. But she was too excited to notice it. She rushed up to her father and cried: "Father, but why are you so late?"

"Forgive me, Mo," said her father, "but we got into a cosmic dust cloud."

"Jeepers creepers," cried Mo. "That is ugh, eek, horrible."

Her father looked at her dumbfounded. But now Mo was jabbering at him in her Asra language.

"Mo," said her father, "let's talk in the human language. It isn't polite when the humans can't understand what we're saying."

"I'm dying of hunger," said Mo. "Do you have a pill?"

Her father gave her one, and Mo gobbled it up. At once she became vivacious and cheerful and called: "Oh, Father, how glad I am to see you again!"

Her father now looked at her more closely and cried out in astonishment: "Mo, how you look! Earth doesn't appear to have agreed with you!" Mo really looked a fright, what with the bruise on her forehead, the scratches on her arm, and the scrape on her knee. Her shoes and socks were gone, as was her coat. Her hair was all tousled and full of pine needles, and, to make things worse, her dress was torn in shreds.

"Earth is quite nice," said Mo. "The air is very thick."

"But where is your coat?" her father asked her.

"Please don't scold," Mo begged. "We had to use it to save Konrad. He could not squeeze through the gap. But he is a good human."

"And where are your shoes and socks?" her father asked.

"They floated away. But it really is not Otto's fault," said Mo.

"Your dress is all torn," her father said.

Mo looked at her dress in consternation. "Holy catfish!" she exclaimed, dismayed. "Now the doll will not have anything to wear any more!"

Her father laughed, and the parents and neighbors joined in. They no longer felt quite as frightened. The people from Asra seemed to be peaceful creatures.

"What happened to your arm, Mo?" asked her father. "It is covered with bloody scratches."

"They were little trees, which scratched and pricked," said Mo.

"Well, you seem to have had many adventures in so short a time," her father said.

"Sure, sure," Mo nodded cheerfully. "We always had to run away and hide."

"Why?" her father asked, astonished.

"The big humans did not believe that I came from Asra," said Mo, and fixed the parents and neighbors with a reproachful eye.

"You shouldn't blame them for that," her father said. "How could they know that we exist on Asra?"

"But I kept telling them so!" Mo called out.

"You're only a little girl, after all," her father said.

"The children saved me!" Mo told her father. "Walter always believed firmly that I came from Asra."

"*Those* children there?" asked the father, and looked at them with curiosity.

"Yes, Father," Mo said with a radiant smile. "And just imagine," she went on, bubbling over, "Erna fell into a swamp hole; Willy was very sick—his nose was bleeding; Otto almost was bitten by an animal with no legs; and I cried—in a church!"

"Cried?" her father asked incredulously. "But you've never cried before!"

"I learned that on Earth," Mo said proudly.

"You seem to have learned a lot on Earth since this morning," her father said, amused.

186

"I also stole an apple, Father, and let the chickens free. And I climbed over a fence," Mo reported excitedly.

"Well, you did not exactly show off your best side," her father remarked, shaking his head.

"Miss Tim is a teacher," Mo said quickly. "She has a canary bird. She wanted to cage me in too!"

"I didn't want to cage you in at all, child," Miss Tim objected laughingly.

Mo's father winked at her reassuringly. "Why did Miss Tim want to lock you up, Mo?" he asked.

"She thought that I rolled my eyes and that I ran with no clothes on through the streets. I never do that, do I, Father?" said Mo.

"No," smiled Mo's father. "Besides, we have no streets."

"And then we climbed up a mountain," Mo continued,

"and we were very licked. And Lottie dreamed of potato soup. Isn't Lottie sweet? And Otto's glasses stank, and . . ."

Mo wanted to tell a great deal more, but her father broke in to say: "Mo, you can tell me about it all on the way! We will have to leave now; otherwise we'll never get back to Asra."

"Oh, good heavens!" exclaimed Mo, and clapped her hands. "I'm probably talking too much baloney!"

"Now say good-by to the children and thank them for all their help," said her father.

Mo went up to the children and shook hands with each of them, just as she had learned to do on earth. "So long, Willy! I thank you! So long, Erna. I thank you! So long, Gretel. I thank you! So long, Lottie. I thank you!" she said each time.

Lottie began to weep. "Sooh-llong!" she sobbed. "Do you really have to leave so soon?"

Walter was the last in line for the handshake. "So long, Walter. I thank you!" She hesitated, then added quickly, "I like you very much!" and then ran to her father. He took her by the hand and walked toward the space ship.

"Mo, Mo!" Walter suddenly shouted frantically. "Your necklace! Your necklace!" He pulled it out of his pocket and waved it in the air. He was shocked that he almost had forgotten to return it to her.

"Good Lord!" called out the neighbors. "The necklace worth a million!"

"And the lad just carries it around in his pants pocket!" Mr. Hofer stammered, completely bewildered.

Mo and her father stopped. Mo was talking to him at a great rate, and several times they turned to look at Walter. Then Mo quickly climbed into the space ship.

Her father came back. "Are you Walter?" he asked.

Walter nodded and handed him the necklace.

"You may keep the necklace," said Mo's father. "Mo wants to give it to you."

"*Oh*," groaned the neighbors, overcome. Mr. and Mrs. Brenner were stunned. Miss Beck, who meanwhile had come to, almost passed out again, except this time out of envy.

"I cannot keep the necklace," stuttered Walter. "Isn't it worth a million?"

"Mo shall get another one from me," her father said.

"I—I can't accept it," Walter protested, in a faint stammer.

"But don't you want to help your parents?" asked Mo's father. "Mo told me that they are poor. You could sell the necklace."

"You really want me to have it?" Walter asked, not trusting his ears.

"Yes," said Mo's father. "It would make Mo very happy."

"Oh, I thank you very much!" said Walter and sighed.

"Only you must promise me to give something really nice to your friends who helped you so wonderfully," said Mo's father. "Agreed?"

"You bet," said Walter, with a full heart. "And again thank you ever so much."

"I must thank *you*," Mo's father said cordially. "You steadfastly believed in my daughter. But for that I might never have seen her again. And I thank you too, children!" he called to the others.

Otto and Willy bowed, while Gretel and Erna curtsied. Only Konrad stood planted like a nitwit. It all was just too much for him.

Mo's father now motioned to the police sergeant, and Mr. Klotz limped up in a hurry.

"You're the police?" Mo's father asked sternly.

"At your service, your excellency!" stammered the sergeant. "Chief sergeant of the district police Klotz reporting, sir!" He stood at attention and even snapped his hand to his bald head in a military salute. He did not even notice that he was still holding his cap in the other hand.

"Sergeant, you are witness to the fact that this young man has legally received this necklace as a present! Is that understood?" Mo's father said crisply.

"At your service, yes, sir, your excellency!" blurted the sergeant, his eyes nearly popping out of their sockets with subservience.

"All right," Mo's father said in a somewhat more friendly tone. "And from now on you'll be very kind to the children. They are good children."

"At your service, yes, sir!" cried the sergeant obediently.

"Good-by, children!" said Mo's father. "Good-by!" he called to the crowd and turned to walk away.

"Just a moment, please, Mr. Kalumba!" begged Miss Tim nervously. "It just so happens that I have a few books with me. I intended to take them home. Perhaps you don't have enough to read on your long trip, and I thought . . ." She quickly pulled three books from her knapsack and gave them to Mo's father.

"Most kind of you," said Mo's father, and accepted the books with obvious pleasure. "But I won't be able to return them soon, as I shall not be back for another fifty years."

"Oh, that's quite all right," said Miss Tim. "I can wait. The books belong to me."

"Many thanks!" said Mo's father, and gave her a hearty handshake. Then he hastened to his space ship. He signaled to his friends, who had been standing patiently near their ships. They stepped aboard, and almost at once the space ships took to the air like rockets and soon disappeared. Mo's father now climbed in, but his space ship at first rose slowly. A porthole opened, and Mo leaned out. Her father stood behind her, holding onto her with an iron grip lest she fall out again.

Mo took off her cap and cheerfully waved to the children. "Yoohoo! Yoohoo! Yoohoo!" she called, but then the space ship began to pick up more and more speed. Soon it was nothing but a fiery dot, which finally vanished.

"Mummy! Mummy!" Gretel cried, and embraced her in ecstasy. "Now we're rich and famous!"

"Will we, too, have roast goose for Sunday dinner?" Lottie peeped excitedly.

"Roast goose every day!" shouted Gretel, and stuck out her tongue at Otto.

Walter held the diamond necklace in his hand and stared at the sky without moving. "We'll have to pay the farmer's wife for the chickens," he murmured. But his thoughts were somewhere else.